MELT

———

KAYLA PARENT

Dedicated to my wonderful friend and Editor, Laura Apgar, who believed in this book when I didn't, and who went above and beyond every step of the way to make my dreams a reality.

OTHER WINTER STANDALONES

PROLOGUE

"I hate Christmas. And I hate all of you!"

The back door slams behind me so hard, the sound seems to echo off the moon. But I don't look back. I run full speed into the Vermont wilderness, wanting to get as far away from my family and this cabin as possible.

How can they act like everything's okay? Why haven't they even mentioned his name? Isn't there a gaping hole in their chests too? Mine first appeared as a sliver of worry when my dad got sick, but when he died this past summer, it morphed into a painful crater, and I haven't been able to breathe since. It's been hard enough surviving these past few months without him, but at Christmas? It's nearly impossible.

My dad *loved* Christmas. He always told me that while Christmas was a day for miracles, Christmas Eve was a night for magic. And my dad had a thing for magic. Not the wand-waving kind, but the sort of magic you feel on the edge of your subconsciousness, or as a small tease in your gut. Magic that got your imagination flowing, and helped you see the world from a different perspective. I've never felt that kind of magic before, but I know it's out there, because I believe in my dad.

Tonight is Christmas Eve. And because of my dad, I'm still looking for that magic. I was clinging to the hope I'd find it up here in Vermont—his favorite place—but I can't feel it anywhere. I can't feel *him* anywhere.

I let my anger and sadness fuel me as I race deeper and deeper into the woods. Normally I'd be scared to be out here at this time of night, but nothing matters anymore. Running face first into the darkness doesn't mean a thing when you've been living without any light.

My mom calls for me, but I don't stop. Tears blur my vision, but I don't slow down. The red party dress I didn't want to wear snags on a branch, but I just pump my legs faster. I don't care that it's ruined. Everything else is.

Something looming ahead catches my eye and I start to slow down. It's a large Vermont elm—the same as the one in the painting we have hanging above our mantel in the living room back at home. Trees were one of my dad's favorite things to paint.

It's the perfect place to stop and be alone for a second. But as I get closer, I realize that someone is already sitting at its roots. My heart jolts with fear, but then it settles when I realize that the person is just a boy around my age. The moon is bright tonight, and I can just make out his features. Or, at least, I can see that he looks about as happy as I do. He's plopped on the ground with his shoulders sagging and his head propped in his hands.

Curiosity, interest, and something else I can't quite describe pass through me, and without thinking, I reach for the camera hanging around my neck and snap his photo. My dad got it for me last Christmas, and I never go anywhere without it.

The flash is loud and bright in the inky darkness, and his head immediately snaps up.

"What do you think you're doing?" he asks, clearly annoyed.

I back up a step. "Sorry, I wasn't trying to bother you. I take pictures of everything—"

"You can't just take a person's picture without permission!"

"You're right. I'll delete it. Sorry."

I make a show of deleting the photo, but I don't really. I know it's wrong, but for some reason, I can't get myself to press that button.

When I look back up, he's glaring at me. "Who are you, anyway?" he asks.

"My name's Birdie. My family rented Mistletoe Cabin for Christmas."

His eyes narrow. "No shit. Really?"

"Have you heard of it?" I ask, confused.

"Everyone's heard of it. It's got to be the biggest house in the whole state."

"Oh."

An awkward silence descends as we take each other in. His hair is dark and pretty short, but there's a wayward curl falling directly in the middle of his forehead. He has large brown eyes and thick, sharp eyebrows that make him look angry. I squirm a little under his gaze, not used to such intensity.

"What are you doing out here?" he asks, still sounding annoyed. "It's nearly midnight."

His tone finally gets to me and my hackles rise. "I could ask you the same question."

For a moment, we scowl at each other, as if neither of us want to break.

But finally he sighs and looks away. "I'm thinking."

"Oh." Suddenly nervous, my reply tumbles out. "I was running and I saw this tree. I was just going to sit down and rest for a while."

"This is *my* thinking tree," he replies. "I'm not on some fancy vacation. I actually live here. And I'd like to be alone."

Our eyes meet and lock, and all the hurt and frustration from the past few months comes rushing forward. To my horror, my lip starts quivering and my eyes water. The last thing I want is for this boy to see me crying, so I turn, prepared to run off. But before I can take a step, his voice stops me.

"Wait, I'm sorry. I've just had a really bad day."

I almost leave without responding. But the hurt in his voice is something I can relate to. So after wiping my face, I turn back around. "It's okay. I've had a bad day too."

He regards me for a moment. Those laser-focused eyes take in my ripped party dress and tearstained face. My cheeks pink again under the scrutiny, and I can't help but wonder what he's thinking. After a moment, he pats the space beside him. After a beat, I walk forward.

"I'm Chase." A gloved hand appears in my line of vision as I sit down. "I live above the pastry shop in town. Well, if you can even call it a town. It's not much to look at these days."

I shake his hand. "Hi, Chase. I'm Birdie. I like your thinking tree. Thanks for sharing it."

This gets a smile out of him, and I feel my cheeks go from pink to red. His smile softens his whole face. It's like nothing I've ever seen—curved up on one side but flat on the other.

"So what are you thinking about?" I ask.

As if a thundercloud has just moved in over his head, his

whole body tenses and his shoulders curl up around himself. "I don't know if I want to say. It's pretty embarrassing and you'd probably just laugh. Everyone else did."

"I wouldn't laugh. My mother always tells me I'm a great listener."

She says this because I used to sit and listen to my father's stories for hours on end. He loved to talk, and I loved to watch him talk. The thought of my father brings a fresh wave of tears to my eyes, but I force myself back into the moment.

Chase side-eyes me, and I know he's deciding whether or not he wants to share. After a long moment of silence, he sighs, putting his head back in his hands. "My girlfriend broke up with me today."

"On Christmas Eve?!" I gasp.

"That's not even the worst part."

Okay, this is getting good. "What's the worst part?"

He rubs his hands over his cheeks, then wiggles his fingers. It's obvious that this is the part he's worried I'll laugh at. I clamp my mouth shut, determined not to make a peep no matter what it is.

"She broke up with me because ... she said I'm a bad kisser."

Oh my God. "Wow. Are you?"

His head snaps to me, offended. "No!"

"Oh."

He huffs out a breath. "I thought *she* was a bad kisser too, but I didn't go tellin' everyone about it."

"She told everyone?!" I'm scandalized.

"Everyone."

"Whoa."

I don't know what else to say. These are problems I don't have. Chase looks totally miserable, and I don't blame him. If that happened to me, I'd probably switch schools.

I reach out and put a hand on his arm. "I don't know much about kissing, so I can't help you there. But I don't think you should worry about this girl. She sounds mean. So even if the kiss had been a good one, she'd probably just be mean about something else eventually. You should find a nice girl to date instead."

He blinks at me. "You're right. She is mean. I don't even really like her that much."

I nod once, then settle back into the tree. "Then you shouldn't think about her. Especially on Christmas Eve."

He smiles that curved smile at me again. "Okay, I won't."

A light snow starts to fall around us. I hold open my palm, catching a few flakes on my fingertips.

"So why were you running?" he asks. "Guy trouble?"

"No. I don't have a boyfriend."

He seems surprised by this. "What do you have to be sad about, then? If your family rented a place like Mistletoe Cabin, you're probably getting some decent gifts this year."

I debate on whether or not to tell him. It's hard for me to talk about my dad without crying. But Chase just opened up to me, so I guess I should return the favor. I turn to him, focusing on the curl on his forehead. "This is my first Christmas without my dad. He died over the summer."

He sucks in a breath. "Shit."

"And that's not even the worst part."

"What's the worst part?" he asks, his voice notably softer.

"I was with him when he died. He told me he loved me, and I didn't say it back. I wanted to, but I was so scared that I couldn't get the words out. I froze, and then he was gone. I was too late."

I close my eyes, thinking of the moment right before he

drifted away forever. His eyes were fading but they locked on mine with strength I know he didn't have. And then he spoke his last words: "Don't ... forget the ... magic. It's in the woods ..." He squeezed my hand while I blinked away tears. "I love you ... Bird."

He held on for a few more seconds. A few more precious moments so I could respond, but I froze, already terrified of a future without him.

"Shit," Chase says again.

"My family doesn't even know it happened. And I was running away from them tonight because I just couldn't handle all the celebrating without my dad. Everyone was exchanging presents and laughing like everything's normal, but things will never be normal again. No one was even talking about him—not even my cousin Dasha, and she knows how sad I've been. All she cares about is the new camera I got her."

I bring my knees up and hide my face, not wanting Chase to see the fresh wave of tears filling my eyes.

"I'm an idiot," he says after a moment.

"Huh?"

"My problem is so dumb compared to yours. Here I am going on and on about some girl, and you actually have a real reason to be sad. I'm an idiot."

A small laugh escapes me. "You're not an idiot."

"And you're right, you know."

I peek up at him. "About what?"

He leans down so he's looking into my eyes. The intensity of his stare ensures that I don't look away. "That Christmas will never be normal for you again. But that's okay, because there's no such thing as normal. Things in life change all the time. You just have to do your best to stay in the moment. That's what my mom says to me, anyway."

I sniffle, wiping under my eyes. "I don't how to do that."

"Here. I'll show you."

He holds out his hand, letting some snow fall into it. He watches it intently, then looks back up at me.

"You see?" he says.

"See what?"

"Before each snowflake melts, there's a split second where you can just make out its design. It happens real quick, but if you focus hard enough, you can catch it. Sometimes when something good is happening, you have to pause to notice it. You have to live in that feeling for a second." He shrugs. "I think that's what my mom means by staying in the moment."

I stare at him, then hold my hand out, letting tiny snowflakes fall into the center of my palm. When I focus on them, I realize Chase is right. For a brief moment, I'm able see the unique pattern of each snowflake before they're gone. It feels like slowing down time. It's beautiful. It's …

"Magic," I say to Chase.

"Yeah. I mean, it's not going to make the loss of your dad hurt any less. But this way, you can still smile at something in the here and now. Enjoy the little things as much as you can. You'll be okay."

I look out at the snow falling around us. There are millions of snowflakes. Millions of chances for something good to happen. No, things won't be normal again. And I'll always miss my dad. But maybe I'll find a new normal eventually. Maybe I can collect enough small moments to feel more like myself.

I turn to Chase, feeling more hopeful than I have in months. "Thank you."

He smiles that smile at me again, and this time, it makes something inside me flutter. But before he can say anything else, I throw myself into his arms, wanting him to know that I'm so much more grateful than words can express. He's given me the first breath of fresh air I've had since my father passed.

After a second, he lifts his arms and hugs me back. He feels like fire on a cold night, and I snuggle into him a little. Then I do as he instructed and close my eyes, basking in the moment. I know instinctively it's a hug that I'll never forget.

"You can tell your dad you love him any time, you know," he says softly. "I'm sure he's listening."

That's true. I tilt my head up, looking up at the stars. "I love you, Dad," I whisper to the wind.

I close my eyes, imaging my dad is there and listening. Something tells me that he is, and more relief pours into me.

Chase suddenly stiffens in my arms.

"What is it?" I ask, pulling back.

"Don't move," he whispers.

Fear ratchets through me at his tone. "What is it?"

"There's a reindeer behind you. It's staring right at us."

A reindeer? In Vermont? Holding my breath, I twist around slowly, and the sight of the enormous, majestic creature floods my field of vision. "That's not a reindeer," I whisper quietly, completely in awe. "It's a moose!"

The moose suddenly makes a throaty grunting sound at the same time it takes a few steps forward. I open my mouth to scream, but Chase clamps his hand around it.

"Don't make a sound," he whispers. "I heard moose can be vicious."

I nod, keeping my wide eyes on the moose.

"Back away slowly," Chase says as we rise to our feet. "Now when I say run, just ... RUN!"

I don't even think. I just start sprinting through the

forest as fast as I can. Chase stays by my side, even though I'm sure he's faster than me. After a few minutes I look behind us, but luckily the moose didn't follow. It's quiet, but my chest is heaving so hard that I start laughing. Chase is beside me, and when he hears me, he starts laughing too. We must look ridiculous, laughing and running in the woods together.

I stop and lean against a tree, unable to stop giggling. "I can't believe you called it a reindeer. Don't you live here? You must see moose all the time."

Chase is still laughing too, his dark eyes bright with mirth. "I don't know. It's Christmas! Reindeer on the brain. You would have made the same mistake."

"No way. My dad loved moose. They were one of his favorite things to paint. There's paintings of Vermont moose all over my house."

We both start laughing again, but when our eyes lock, and the laughter drifts away with the wind.

Something strange happens in the next few seconds. It's impossible, but it feels like the moment is physically closing in on us. Despite the weather, a warm chill washes over my skin, and a shimmery sound starts up in my ears. It's scary but wonderful, and I've never felt anything like it.

I don't know Chase. I just met him fifteen minutes ago, but deep in my gut, I know there's something inside him that has intrinsically connected to something inside of me. It could be the intensity of his gaze and the way it makes me feel. Or it could be the fact that he gave me hope for my future, and my soul is grateful for it. But something tells me that's not everything. There's something unexplainable here too. When I realize what it is, my heart pounds like a drum.

"Magic ..."

For the first time in my life, I feel magic.

Chase's answering smile tells me that I must have said the word out loud. He nods, as if he knows what I mean. "I feel it too."

He takes a few steps toward me, and when he reaches for my hand, I don't stop him. Even through our gloves, I can sense the buzzing of his skin as his hand connects with mine.

When we lock eyes this time, something intangible forms between us and clicks into place.

I know we're going to kiss before it happens. He moves in closer, and just before our lips touch, I picture a snowflake. I close my eyes and drift into that moment between breaths, basking in the sweet anticipation of what's about to happen to me—my first kiss.

When his lips finally touch mine, I'm already floating high.

I've imagined being kissed a thousand times, but it didn't prepare me for the enormity of the real thing. For the first few seconds, I freeze, just like I always do. But Chase is patient. His lips move slowly across mine, encouraging and enticing me forward at my own pace. Something inside me starts to melt, and I finally press my lips back against his, wanting more of the glorious high that's releasing inside me.

Our mouths move together in a dreamlike state, and in my head, I see bursts of flickering stars. Kissing Chase is enchanting, and my whole body is hyper-focused on him and the new sensations coursing through me. I move closer at the same time he does, our newly formed connection growing stronger by the second. Our lips start moving in sync, seamless, as if we've kissed a thousand times. When his tongue swipes across my lower lip, it leaves a trail of fire and something in my heart changes. Like the little girl inside of it has grown taller and wiser.

I open my mouth wider, wanting to let him in—

"BIRDIE! WHERE ARE YOU?!"

Chase and I rip apart, both gasping for breath. The air around us is still thick and alive, and I wonder for a second if I imagined my cousin's voice.

"BIRDIE!"

Nope. That's definitely her. I shake my head to try to clear the fog. "It's Dasha. My cousin."

"Oh ... okay," he manages, swallowing audibly.

I'm suddenly shy. Overwhelmed. I have no idea what to do or say, like I'm back to being frozen. But I still smile, because above all, I'm happy. And it's all because of Chase.

Backing away, I give him a different smile. One that feels foreign on my face. A woman's smile, maybe. He responds by smiling back, and I know that I'll compare every other smile to his from here on out.

"BIRDIE! WHERE ARE YOU?!"

"I've got to go."

His mouth is moving as if he can't get words out fast enough. Like he, too, is freezing. What a turn the night has taken! What a change I have made. I feel like a new person.

So just before I turn to go, I say something bold.

"Merry Christmas, Chase. You're definitely not a bad kisser."

1

NINE YEARS LATER

Isn't it wonderful how you can feel a holiday in the air?

It's the night before Thanksgiving, and everyone on campus is getting ready for a few days off. Students are bustling around the cafeteria with a different sort of energy guiding their steps. Smiling, I slow down and take it all in, letting their excitement, and the moment, wash over me.

My boyfriend's voice, however, brings me back to reality.

"All the high-ranking executives from my dad's company are going to be there, so we're going all out," Rhett says proudly. He grins at me, squeezing my leg under the table. "Normally I hate Thanksgiving, but this year, it's going to be the shit."

"I wish I could go," Janice pouts, shooting me an accusatory look. "Bird, as my best friend, you should have told me your man was throwing the Thanksgiving of the century. Maybe I can get out of Thanksgiving at my house. You know, tell my mom something came up."

"You can't stand up your own mother," I scold gently,

knowing she would actually do it. "But how about I bring the two of you some dessert afterward? I'd love to see her."

"Yeah, sure. Scraps for us little people," she grumbles.

"Don't say that," I say, giving her a look.

Truth is, I'd love to trade places with Janice. An intimate family Thanksgiving sounds a lot better than a fifty-plus-person affair with people I don't even know. But I don't dare say that out loud. This night is all Rhett has been talking about for weeks, and I don't want to rock the boat.

"Speaking of dessert," Rhett cuts in, smiling at me. "I have a surprise for you, baby. You're going to be in for a real treat, literally."

"Can't wait," I tell him, doing my best to feign enthusiasm. Rhett's surprises are never about me. Not really. Some way or another, they also somehow benefit him. Like the time he got me the crock pot for Christmas, and a book of recipes with his favorites earmarked. I've learned to live with it at this point, but it's getting harder and harder to pretend it doesn't bug me.

"And you did tell your mom it's black-tie, right?" he asks. "I don't want her showing up in khakis like she did on my birthday."

"She knows," I respond patiently. "We've both got gowns picked out."

"Ugh. Gorgeous gowns, surprise desserts, important people drinking champagne out of crystal glasses—must be nice to have money," Janice says, looking between us. "I'll be lucky if my mom comes to the table with her hair combed."

Rhett laughs, but I frown. Janice is really laying it on thick today.

"Your mom is so much fun around the holidays," I tell her, trying to lift her spirits. "Remember when we all snuggled around her keyboard, singing carols? That was the best version of 'Jingle Bells' I've ever heard."

Janice doesn't respond. She just rolls her eyes, poking at her food.

"Anyway, I've got to run," Rhett says, oblivious. "I'll see you tonight." He leans over and pecks my lips. "Later, Janice."

"See you, Rhett," she says, smiling up at him.

My body sags with relief once he walks away. All the bragging he's been doing about his event is getting old. I swear, if I hear another word about how expensive everything will be, or about all the important people who are going to be there, I am going to scream. Not to mention, I told him not to bring it up anymore in front of Janice, but of course he couldn't help himself. That's Rhett. When he gets excited about something, he goes all in. Like a little kid, his joy is contagious and consuming. But the flip side of the coin is that he can be pretty unaware of anything other than himself.

"You're so lucky," Janice gripes again, getting my attention.

"You're really not going to be missing much," I tell her, exasperated. "It's going to be a bunch of stuffy old men patting themselves on the back all night and eating over-priced lobster."

"Not because of that." She points her fork in the direction Rhett walked off. "But because I can totally tell that he is going to be proposing to you soon."

I stiffen, looking down at my tray. "You don't know that."

"Oh, please. He's been dropping some seriously obvious hints. My guess is he does it at the Christmas party. That's your favorite holiday and you know how he likes to make big romantic gestures."

My stomach churns at the thought. It's not that I don't love Rhett—I do. But I'm not sure I'm ready to be engaged to him. And Janice is right. He's been making it pretty obvious that he wants to put a ring on my finger. He keeps making little comments about taking the next step after graduation, and how the past three years we've been together have been the best of his life.

"I just don't know if I'm ready," I admit quietly. "We're still so young."

"We're seniors, Bird. About to enter the real world." She narrows her eyes at me. "And unlike the rest of us, you'll get to do it with a giant rock on your finger."

"It's not just our age ..." I look at Janice carefully, and then decide to tell her something that's been on my mind for a while. "I just ... I'm not sure about Rhett. Aren't you supposed be totally sure before you agree to spend the rest of your life with someone?"

She looks like at me like I've got two heads. "How can you not be sure? Rhett's rich, he's probably the hottest guy on campus, and he's on a one-way track to becoming a top investor at his dad's company."

"I'm not saying he's not a good catch—"

"Good catch? Guys like that are *the* catch." She shakes her head. "Any girl would be lucky to have Rhett. Maybe you should try appreciating what you have for once."

"I'm just saying—"

"I've got to go," she cuts in, gathering her books.

"Janice, come on, don't go. I'm sorry."

"It's fine, just forget it. Have a good Thanksgiving." Before I can say another word, she storms away from table, leaving me a bit shell-shocked.

It's not the first time she's snapped at me in the past couple of months. Janice and I have been best friends since middle school, but she's had a chip on her shoulder ever since the semester started. I know her well enough to know she's nervous about graduating, but I don't know why she's taking it out on me. I want to say something to her about it, but it seems that every time I try, she jumps down my throat.

My phone buzzes with a text just as I'm throwing out my food.

Mom: A little bird told me the Holiday Photo Contest starts today. Good luck!

The news instantly lifts my mood. I've been waiting for this contest for what seems like a lifetime. I rush out of the cafeteria, feeling a little bit of that holiday energy.

2

————

I meet Dasha outside our photography class. When she sees the excitement on my face, she instantly smiles. That's the wonderful thing about Dasha. If you're happy about something, she's immediately happy too—without even knowing what it is.

"Okay, spill." She giggles when I stop in front of her. "I know you love photography, but you're not usually one to literally run to class."

"Holiday Photo Contest starts today!" I all but squeal. "Officially."

She lights up just like I did. "Seriously?! I figured he'd wait to announce it after Thanksgiving break."

"Nope. My mom just told me." I have no idea how she found out, but she and my father both went to this college back in the day, so she probably still has a few contacts here and there.

Dasha bounces on her toes. "I can't believe we're seniors and can finally enter. I wonder what the parameters will be? I hope something to do with clothing like last year. That gallery was amazing."

I, of course, am hoping for an outdoor theme. While Dasha loves taking portraits and photographing people, I love landscapes, just like my father loved painting them. I used to watch him for hours, fascinated by how the scenery came together stroke by stroke.

"I think it's going to be something big," I say. "It's the fiftieth anniversary this year, so it's got to be special."

"Well, let me be the first to tell you good luck. I just know you're going to capture something incredible."

"Thanks, Dasha. You too."

Despite our mutual love of photography, there's no ill will or competitiveness between us. When my dad bought me my first camera, I fell in love with photography instantly. Wanting to share that, I gifted Dasha her first camera the next year, and I'm so happy that I did. Our styles are completely different, and the fact that we've been able to bounce ideas and share photos with each other over the years has been nothing but a positive experience. And after being around Janice so much lately, Dasha's attitude is like a breath of fresh air.

Professor Donovan opens the door and waves us all in. "Find your seats, everyone. Big day today."

Dasha and I hustle inside and take our seats in the front row. Looks like my mom was right. The words *Holiday Photo Contest, 50th Anniversary* are written on the whiteboard in big bold letters. Now it's not just Dasha and me who are excited. There's a low hum in the room and everyone is whispering to one another. I take a moment to close my eyes and enjoy the anticipation. I've waited for this moment. It's going to be my first true opportunity to make my dad proud.

Professor Donovan walks to the front of the room and leans against his desk. He looks around, smiling, and I know he's just as excited as we are.

"Okay, okay, settle down everyone," he says.

Because of his impeccable delivery of critique and support, he's one of my favorite professors. He's not half bad to look at either. He has flawless dark brown skin, a wide smile and kind eyes that seem to wink at you. But more importantly, he's an incredible photographer and I've learned so much from him over the years.

"Today's the day, folks," he continues. "I know a lot of you have been waiting years for this, so without further ado, I'd like to announce that the 50th County-Wide Holiday Photo Contest is officially under way."

Every single person in the lecture hall breaks out into excited chatter. The sound carries around the room, building in volume until it's near deafening. There are probably one hundred and fifty of us here who are eligible to enter, and even more on the neighboring campuses.

"As you all know, the contest is open to seniors only, specifically to those who have passed at least three of our advanced courses. You must submit your photo by the twenty-third of December, and the winner—chosen by a small team of professionals—will be announced on Christmas Eve."

He pauses for emphasis, the smile on his face widening. "As is tradition, the winner will get his or her own private gallery opening at the Smithwise in Hartford, and five thousand dollars in prize money."

The class erupts again, and this time, I join them. I don't care about the money, and while the gallery opening is an incredible opportunity, it's also not the main reason I'm so anxious to win.

My father, Roy Tenneson, had always been revered as a creative genius. And by the end of his career, he was a world-renowned artist. He traveled the world painting his landscapes, and was respected and celebrated in the most elite of art communities. Painting was his bread and butter, but he was also talented with a camera. In fact, back when he was a student, he won the 28th[th] Annual Holiday Photo Contest with a photo he took near Mistletoe Cabin.

It's always been my goal to follow in his footsteps and make him proud. Even though he's no longer here, winning this contest and validating my art is still important to me.

"What's the theme this year?" someone asks.

"Ah, and now we get to the fun part," Professor Donovan replies. "In years past, there have been strict guidelines. Themes such as 'holiday cooking' and 'fun in the snow' gave students a solid jumping-off point for their submissions. But this year, in honor of the fiftieth anniversary, the theme is broad and simple. The judges want to see your individual versions of the perfect holiday photo."

Dasha and I share a look. The *perfect* holiday photo? What does that even mean? How are we supposed to work with that?

"Now, you may be wondering..." Professor Donovan continues. "How can one judge what is perfect and what's not, especially when the holidays mean different things for different people?"

That's exactly what I'm wondering.

"But that's the beauty of the word 'perfect.' It is, in and of itself, flawed. If I had to give you some advice, I'd say go for authenticity. Find your own perfect. Be true to yourself, and let that shine through in your submission."

I stare the board, my mind racing. How can I portray perfect at Christmastime? Should I take a quintessential photo of a family baking cookies together? A father and son sledding down a hill? A star being placed on top of a Christmas tree? Maybe a Christmas/Hanukkah/Kwanzaa mash-up? The possibilities are endless. I don't even know where to start. Over the past three years, whenever I heard the guidelines but couldn't enter, I knew exactly the photo I'd take for it. But of course, now, when it's go time, I'm coming up empty.

By the end of class, I'm still no closer to an idea. But I have over three weeks, and I'm confident I'll think of something. At least, I hope I will. The stakes are too high for the alternative.

I'm one of the last students to leave the room, and Professor Donovan stops me on my way out the door.

"So what do you think, Birdie? Got any ideas for the contest? I know how much you've been looking forward to this."

Does he ever. I probably asked three times this semester alone when he'd be announcing it. "Not yet," I reply. "But I'm not totally in the Christmas mood right now. Maybe after Thanksgiving, something will come to me."

He grins. "You know, the theme the year your dad won was holiday pairs. He submitted a beautiful photograph of a moose standing next to your mother."

"I know the photo well," I say. "Talk about perfect."

It's a photo of my mom in a red dress standing next to a tall pine tree. A few feet away is the largest moose my parents both said they've ever seen. They're staring at each other, and my mom is reaching her hand out. She's smiling, and I swear it looks like the moose is smiling too. With Vermont mountains in the back, the photo is breathtaking.

"It's a wonderful photo," he agrees. "Although I don't think your mom was a fan, if I remember correctly?"

"Nope," I say, smiling. "She thinks she looks like some crazy forest lady."

We both laugh, and a warm feeling settles into my chest.

Professor Donovan and I talk about my parents often. The three of them attended this university at the same time and were in a few of the same classes. It's nice to have someone to talk about my dad with. They weren't exactly friends, but then again, my dad didn't really have time for friends. He was always wrapped up in his work, brainstorming his next masterpiece.

"Good luck, Birdie. Enjoy your holiday."

"You too. Happy Thanksgiving."

I'm at the door when he stops me once more. "He'd be proud of you, you know. Your father."

I shoot him one last smile before leaving.

He'd be even more proud of me if I win this contest, I think to myself. So that's what I plan to do, no matter the cost.

3

____

Rhett's Thanksgiving party feels like it's been going on for hours, and we haven't even had dinner yet. I sulk, looking around at the sea of unfamiliar faces. It just seems wrong to spend a holiday with strangers.

Rhett, however, is having the time of his life.

"... and then my dad said, next time, just shoot the turkey your damn self!"

The group of men standing around Rhett and me burst into laughter, so I force out a chuckle. I've heard Rhett tell this story before. It's not that I don't find it funny, I just wish I could excuse myself and go hang out with my mom. I've never been good at making small talk, especially with people I don't know. Rhett, however, made me promise not to leave his side tonight. He said he needed me there for moral support while he schmoozed and networked with his dad's business associates. I'm happy to be supportive, but I've barely been able to get a word in edgewise. The whole thing has me feeling like festive arm candy.

Not to mention, I'm _really_ uncomfortable. I'm in a black floor-length evening gown with matching heels, and since the dress is skin tight, I'm wearing a thong. Trying not to think about the fact that I have the world's biggest wedgie, I smile and sip my champagne.

"Rhett, dear, can I borrow Birdie for a moment?"

I turn to my mom gratefully. Without waiting for Rhett's response, I exit the circle and thread my arm through my mother's. Once we're out of earshot, I sigh with relief.

"Thanks, Mom. I needed that."

"No kidding. I saw you squirming from all the way across the room. Let me guess. A thong?"

I groan. "Whoever said black-tie was a good idea for Thanksgiving, anyway? Mulberry silk and turkey just don't mix."

She lovingly pats my arm. "I agree. Next year, you and I will wear sweatpants, socks, and big granny-panty under-wear while we stuff our faces with our favorite comfort foods."

"Deal," I say on a laugh. "Sounds like heaven."

But my smile quickly fades. Where will I even be next year? Will I be engaged to Rhett? I look around. Is *this* what my holidays will look like from here on out? Being surrounded by people whom I have nothing in common with while I'm dragged around on my husband's arm? The thought is incredibly depressing.

"What is it now?" my mom asks.

"Nothing. Just the thong, like you said."

I'm not ready to tell her how I feel just yet. Probably because I'm not even sure of how I feel. I don't have the words, and I know I'd just bungle it all up if I tried to explain it to her. I just don't understand why I suddenly feel so out of control. Like life is happening to me and there's nothing I can do to slow it down.

"Only a few more hours," she responds. "I'm not exactly comfortable myself."

I give her a look. "You'd never know it."

With her long brown hair, red painted lips, and youthful skin, my mom looks immaculate for her age. Not to mention, she can still rock the hell out of an evening gown.

"I had a lot of practice going to things like this with your father," she says. "We always had some art party to be at or some mogul to meet. It was exhausting."

"I wish Dad was here," I say wistfully, resting my head on her shoulder. "Holidays with him were the best."

Her face softens and she squeezes my arm. "Come on. It looks like dinner is starting."

I meet back up with Rhett at the table. He's in a great mood, so my guess is all the schmoozing he's doing is going well.

"Havin' fun, baby?" he whispers in my ear as he pulls out my chair. The gentleman-like move annoys me, because I know he's only doing it for show.

I wish I could tell him the truth—that I'm not really having fun at all—but I don't want to spoil his big night, so I just smile and nod. "Yeah, everything looks perfect."

He beams with pride. "And we haven't even gotten to the best part."

The best part? Uh oh. My pulse starts racing. Would he propose here? In front of all of these strangers?

I don't know what I'd do. But before I can really start to panic, he puts my fears to rest.

"My tasty surprise," he clarifies.

"Oh." Relief floods me, although my hands are still shaking. "Right. I almost forgot about that. I can't wait."

His leg starts bouncing and he bites his lip. "You know what? Screw it. I'm too excited. I'll just tell you now."

Typical Rhett. Too impatient for his own good. But I fight a smile, watching his face light up. It's endearing to see his youthful excitement for things. "Sure, if you want to," I say.

He leans forward, a big grin on his face. "The company I hired for dessert is going to be my first official investment. Dad's loaning me the capital, and I've pledged to double it by graduation. If all goes well, I'll have made a name for myself before I even start at the firm next summer."

Genuine happiness for him has me smiling from ear to ear. "Rhett, that's wonderful! What company is it? Tell me everything."

"We're working on the name. But the kid who owns it is doing really cutting-edge stuff with dessert, which is why I chose it. There's already a buzz around him up north, so when I was scouring the LLC lists for something new, he stuck out."

"That's amazing." I beam at him. "But dessert? I'm kind of surprised. You don't even really like dessert."

His eyes soften. "Yeah, but you do."

My face falls into a smile. He can be really sweet sometimes. "That's thoughtful, Rhett. I'm really happy for you. I just can't believe you didn't tell me. You must have been working on this for months."

"Like I said, I wanted it to be a surprise." He gives me a meaningful look. "I think you'll see that I'm full of those this year."

He grabs my hand and kisses my ring finger.

Yeah, he's definitely going to propose. He couldn't be making it any more obvious. A real surprise proposal would be too risky for him, so he's letting me know in his own way to prepare for it.

Before my earlier panic can set in, Rhett's father gets everyone's attention to say grace, and the meal begins.

Everything is delicious. I should have known it would be, considering all the bragging Rhett was doing. I'm digging into my third helping of mac n' cheese when I hear my name. I turn my ear to Rhett to listen in on what he's saying.

"Her photographs are really something to see ..."

Aww. My heart lifts. He really is being sweet tonight.

"It's a fun little hobby she's had since she was a little girl. Her father is *the* Roy Tenneson, you know ..."

And just like that, my mood sours. *Hobby.* It's not the first time he's belittled my chosen career path. If I was someone else, I would interrupt and correct him. Or, at least, I'd tell him how much it bothers me when we get home later. But every time I try to stand up for myself, I just freeze. It's like my whole body shuts down. I know he would just talk his way out of it, so why even bother?

I stew for the rest of the meal, but when dessert rolls around, I try to muster up some excitement for him. He's been talking about making his first investment for years, so I know this is a major deal, and whoever he chose must really be something special.

Rhett stands up from the table and taps a fork against his glass to get everyone's attention. "Sorry to interrupt," he begins. "But I have just a couple of things I want to say. For those of you who don't know me, my name is Rhett Branholder, the son of our fearless leader over there. First things first—how about a hand for my parents for that fantastic meal?"

After everyone claps and cheers for the Branholders, Rhett begins again. "As some of you know, I'll be proudly joining the ranks of B&B Investing come next July. But I don't want to arrive empty-handed. Even though I'm the CEO's son, I still want to prove myself worthy to work alongside some of the best minds in the business. Which is why, as of this past spring, I've made my first official investment."

He smiles, waving away some of the cheers before starting to pace the table. "I chose this company not only because of their delicious desserts, but because the owner keeps his finger on the pulse of what's trending. He uses improved baking techniques to create unique sweets like boozy caramels, hot ice cream, and pie on a stick, the latter of which we'll be serving you tonight. And I wanted to go one step further, so I invited him here to dole out these amazing desserts himself. So here he is—the man behind the magic, Chase Cyrus!"

When Rhett gestures to the door that leads to the kitchen, a strange chill sweeps over my skin. It's a sensation that's hard to describe with words, but it feels like the universe is shifting, or the winds of change are whispering to me directly. No, not whispering. Warning.

The door opens, and then as if in slow motion, out walks the boy I've thought about every day for nine years. The boy who gave me two precious gifts the night I ran crying into the Vermont wilderness.

But he's not a boy anymore. He's a man. And he's staring right at me.

4

___

"*E*xcuse me. I have to use the bathroom."

I throw my napkin on my plate and shove back from the table.

Rhett puts a hand on my arm. "Wait, Chase is going to explain some of his methods and the new shop we're opening. Don't go just yet—"

"It's an emergency, sorry."

Looking down at the floor, I book it from the dining room as fast as possible. Despite the chaos inside me, I manage to keep a blank expression, but it's all I can do to make it to the bathroom in once piece.

After closing the door, I rush to the sink. I splash cold water on my face, but it does nothing to dilute the shock of seeing Chase again. That moment we shared in the forest feels like a dream to me. So much so, that I sometimes wonder if I made it all up, or imagined him as a way to cope with my father's loss.

For years afterward, I searched for Chase. But I only had a first name and a tentative location to go on, so I never had any luck. He wasn't on social media and nothing came up in a general search. A few months after Chase and I met, I was able to track down the pastry shop his parents must have owned, but it had since closed with no forwarding number.

Even after all that, I didn't want to give up. So one year on a whim, I took a trip to Vermont. I tried to ask around about him, but no one knew anything. I wandered around aimlessly for days, going in and out of shops, but eventually had to give up.

I didn't think I'd ever find him.

And now, here he is, standing in my boyfriend's dining room.

Even though our eyes met for only a moment, I know he recognized me too. He was smiling when he walked into the room, but when he scanned the crowd and his eyes landed on me, his whole demeanor changed. His face transformed, as if he'd been hit by a shockwave. And his shoulders, they didn't just jump; they shook, like he felt the same chill I did. And those eyes, those dark piercing eyes, went wide with the intensity I still remember from that night.

It was too much for me. The moment was overwhelming; I had to get away.

Now I pace the bathroom and wring my hands. I don't even know what to do with myself right now. Do I just go back out there and pretend everything's normal? Do I greet him like an old friend? Just the thought of talking to him makes my knees weak.

But one thing I can't do is hide in here all night. So after a few long moments, I school my features into some semblance of calm.

I open the door and step into the hallway, but stop short when I realize someone is standing there waiting for me.

Chase.

Time moves in slow motion as we take each other in.

He's still got that intense stare and those piercing brown eyes, and that wayward curl still hangs in the middle of his forehead. But otherwise, he's transformed from the boy I remember. The slightly lanky pre-teen is now a tall, well-muscled man with a confident set to his shoulders that wasn't there before.

But he *feels* the same. My body recognizes his presence, and for a moment, I'm instantly transported back to that night in the forest.

"You," I say softly.

"You." His deep voice sends a shot of awareness over my skin.

"I didn't think I'd ever see you again," I whisper.

"I thought you were a dream."

"I thought the same thing."

It's quiet for a moment as the shimmery bubble wraps around us again.

"I looked for you," he says then, his eyes searching mine. "I must have Googled Birdie one thousand times since that night. I even went as far as to try and get records of who rented Mistletoe Cabin, but they keep that information under lock and key."

"My real name is Beatrice," I tell him. "And I Googled you too. I even went up to Vermont once, but no one had any information on you. All they told me was that your family's pastry shop closed down and no one had heard from any of you since."

He shakes his head as if amazed by this information. "Uh, yeah, we shut our doors right after a few months after we met, and the only social media I've ever had is the new account I just made for my business." He runs a hand over his jaw, astonishment still present on all his features. "I just can't believe it's you. And you look ..." He shakes his head as his eyes take me in from head to toe. "You look"—he repeats, and this time his voice is deeper—"like you really are a dream."

I blush from the tips of my toes to the roots of my hair. "Thank you, Chase. You look great too. And congrats on the business."

He smiles and my heart stutters. It's *the* smile. The curved one I dream about. I thought I remembered it, but my memory pales in comparison to the real thing.

"Thank you," he says. "I started it a few years ago. I've always wanted to follow in my dad's footsteps, and I finally had the opportunity. I was hoping my first shop would be in Vermont, but we found a prime space here in New Haven. It's convenient for now, since it's close to campus. College students are a great market for sweets."

I stare at him, shocked by all this information. "Your shop is in New Haven? And you're going to school around here?"

"Yeah, downtown. I'm just taking a business analytics class at the community college. Are you in school?"

"I study photography at the university. I graduate next year."

"Photography, huh? I remember you said you like to take pictures," he says, smiling.

"Right," I say, blushing, remembering the first few moments we met.

"I'm renting a place right around the university," he tells me. "I pass it on my way to work."

My eyes go wide. "I live around there too."

He makes a noise low in his throat. "Damn. I've been here since September. I can't believe you've been so close to me this whole time."

We stare at each other, both seemingly unable to look away.

"Chase, I ..."

There are so many things I want to say to him. I want to tell him that he didn't just give me my first kiss, he virtually saved me during a really rough time and gave me a whole new way to look at life. Every day, several times a day, I take the time to slow down and live in the moment. I appreciate my surroundings and just *feel*, like he taught me how to do with the snowflake. Those brief and beautiful pauses helped me cope with my father's loss and were instrumental in my healing. I'm a better person because of it. I want to tell him all of this, but the words are frozen in my throat.

"Baby? That you?"

I jump at the sudden burst of our bubble. Rhett's voice sounds like a clatter, and when he comes up beside me, reality comes crashing back in.

"What's going on?" he asks, his gaze swinging between Chase and me.

I make a quick decision. Rhett can't know that this is *the* Chase. I don't even want to think about all the trouble it would cause.

I met Rhett at Janice's Christmas party freshman year, and we immediately hit it off. But when he asked me out, I told him no. The reason was I still thought about Chase and was hoping to find him. That was around the time I went up to Vermont. But when I came back empty-handed, I was convinced I'd never see Chase again, so I told myself to give Rhett a chance.

Rhett knows all of this. So if he knew the truth about who his client was, it wouldn't be good for anyone. Not to mention, the two of them are in business together and I don't want to introduce any sour feelings between the two of them.

"Hey," I say, forcing a casual tone. "Just introduced myself to Mr. Cyrus here. I figured if you two are going to be working together, I should say hello."

Chase gives me a strange look and goes to speak, but then his eyes settle on Rhett's hand, which has wrapped itself around my waist.

I can see the moment it all hits him—the moment he realizes that Rhett and I are dating, and that I don't want him to know about our shared history. A few emotions pass over his face. Confusion. Surprise. Disbelief. But the disappointment is the most apparent—although for what, I don't know.

"That's was nice of you, baby," Rhett says, sliding his hand down over my hip. "See Chase? Didn't I tell you I had the sweetest girlfriend?"

I close my eyes. The awkwardness of this moment is nearly unbearable.

Chase lets the question hang for a little bit longer than he should. "Yeah, you did tell me that once or twice." He looks at me and raises a brow. "I've heard good things."

I just nod in response. I don't think I could speak even if I wanted to.

Rhett turns to me. "Wait until you try his snowflake pudding. It's the best-selling item on his menu. It's like a snow cone and pudding mixed in one. We're going to serve it at the Christmas party."

Snowflake? Is it just a coincidence? Or did he choose snowflakes because that moment in the forest meant as much to him as it did to me?

"Wow," I swallow. "Shaved ice and pudding mixed in one. How do you do it?"

Chase's eyes bore into mine. "With magic."

Magic. Our exchange from that night comes back to me, and I remember whispering the word to him out loud. I know deep in my gut that he's letting me know that no, the name "snowflake pudding" is not a coincidence. He named this dessert with me in mind.

Rhett laughs. I make a noise that's supposed to be laughter, but probably sounds more like choking. "I can't wait to try it," I eventually get out.

"I also really enjoy his holiday mousse," Rhett continues, completely oblivious. "That's my favorite."

"Spelled m-o-o-s-e," Chase adds quietly. "I once saw a moose up in Vermont, so I wanted to pay homage to where I'm from."

"Just once?"

"Just once," Chase confirms, staring directly into my eyes.

It feels like the floor is falling beneath my feet. Chase has made another nod to our night, and this one is even more obvious than the first. Chase and I share another look, and the strength of the moment is suddenly too overwhelming.

I smile up at Rhett. "Sounds delicious. But I won't get to try anything if I'm standing around here, will I?"

Looping my arm with Rhett's, I start pulling him back to the dining room. Rhett says goodbye to Chase over my shoulder, and I think Chase responds, but the low hum in my ear drowns it out.

Before I turn the corner, I chance one more look over my shoulder. There's just something in me that's desperate for one more look at the man that I thought I lost forever.

Chase is staring back at me, his expression riddled with regret.

5

The night after Thanksgiving, as is tradition, Janice, Dasha, my mother and I are putting up Christmas decorations at our house. My dad always loved decorating and insisted we do it the moment Thanksgiving was over, and we've kept up with it ever since. The first year after he died, my mom and I put up the decorations alone. It was incredibly depressing, so the second year my mom invited Dasha and Janice to try to lift my spirits, and it's become a tradition ever since.

As I wrap a string of lights around the tree, I try to stay in the moment, but I just can't get Chase out of my head. Specifically, the way he looked at me when I left him standing there in the hallway keeps flashing in my mind. I've pictured a reunion between us hundreds of times, and this is definitely not how I wanted things to go.

The rest of the night, Chase was busy talking with Rhett's guests and handing out his desserts, so there were no more moments for us to be alone. But there were stolen glances on both sides. I eventually excused myself early and had my mom drive me home.

"Rhett's party sounds like it was incredible," Janice comments, unpacking the ornament box with a little more force than necessary. "I still can't believe I had to miss out."

"Eh," Dasha shrugs, holding up a sparkling red bauble to the light. "The food sounded like it was great, but otherwise, it seemed like a total drag." She cringes, then looks over at me. "No offense."

"None taken. It was sort of a drag."

Well, it was, before the blast from my past.

Janice shakes her head. "Sometimes I really don't understand you two."

Dasha and I share a small smile over her head. Janice loves a good party, especially the fancy ones like Rhett throws. I can only wish I had a little bit of her enthusiasm.

"All right, who wants a hot cocoa?" My mom sweeps into the room and passes out mugs.

The frothy sweet treat reminds me of last night. Chase served a delicious salted vanilla hot chocolate. My mom described it as divine, and she was right. And it wasn't just the taste that was impeccable. The classy, themed mug Chase served it in had a tasteful charm, and he'd tied little trinkets detailing his website and new business address around the handle. All of his desserts were an experience, and I could see why Rhett chose to work with him. He's clearly doing amazing things with his company, and even though I barely know him, I'm proud.

I wish I told him how wonderful it all was, but I was hardly able to face him, let alone—

"Hellooooo. Earth to Birdie!"

I look up at the sound of my mom's voice. She, Dasha, and Janice are all staring at me.

"What? What did I mis?"

Dasha giggles. "Your mom asked if you wanted marsh-mallows, like, three times."

Janice raises a brow. "You've been distracted all night. What's going on with you? And don't say nothing."

My gut reaction is not to tell them. But these three women know me better than anyone in the world, and there's no use trying to hide it. They all know about Chase and how much that moment in the forest meant to me. Dasha in particular is the one who encouraged me to go to Vermont before saying yes to Rhett.

I take a deep breath and put down my mug. "I'm sorry. I just have a lot on my mind. Something ... happened last night."

"I knew it," my mom says, snapping her fingers. You were so quiet toward the end of the night. And you had a look on your face like you'd seen a ghost."

"I did," I whisper. "At least, that's what it felt like."

The room goes quiet.

"What do you mean, Birdie?" Dasha asks, sounding worried. "Are you okay?"

"I'm fine. It's just ... you know the guy we talked about earlier? The one who brought the desserts last night? Chase Cyrus?"

They all nod.

"Well ... he's Chase. *The* Chase."

All three of them gasp, and if I wasn't so emotionally overwhelmed, I would laugh.

"Beatrice Tenneson! How could you not mention some-thing last night?" Mom asks, her jaw on the floor. "And how did I not put this together? I should have known when you ran out of the room the second he was introduced."

"I can't believe this!" cries Dasha. "Chase. *The* Chase."

"Holy crap," Janice whispers, her eyes wide. "He's going to be working with Rhett? What are you going to do?"

I get up and start pacing the snowflake-themed rug we've laid down in living room. "I have no idea what to do. Especially after I spoke to him last night. I really made a mess of things."

All three of them gasp again.

"Oh my God, you talked to him?" squeaks Dasha. "What happened?"

I quickly tell them about our conversation, how I pretended not to know him, and my hasty departure with Rhett.

"But now I feel so guilty," I continue. "I could tell he was hurt and confused about why I was giving him the cold shoulder. There just wasn't a chance to explain."

"Don't be too hard on yourself," my mom says gently. "Seeing him was a shock. You made the best decision you could in the moment."

"I think so too," Dasha says, putting a comforting hand on my shoulder. "I would have done the same thing. Last night wasn't the night to give Rhett a shock like that. He'd flip if he knew it was *the* Chase, and you know how hard he worked to make yesterday perfect. It would have been devastating."

"I know you guys are right," I say. "But I still feel terrible about it. You should have seen Chase's face."

"Then go find him and explain things," my mom suggests. "He'll understand once you tell him your reasoning."

"But how? I don't have his number. I mean, I guess I could look through Rhett's things, but that just feels wrong."

She taps her chin. "You did say he was taking classes at the community college, right?"

I bark out a laugh. "Are you saying I should just show up there and hope to see him? He'll think I'm a stalker."

"I think he'd want to see you," my mom replies.

"I think so too," Dasha agrees. "And I think you'll feel a lot better about the whole thing if you talk to him."

I can't deny the thought of seeing him again is tempting. "Yeah, I think I would. I guess ... I guess that's what I'll do, then. First thing next week."

Janice suddenly drops a handful of ornaments on the table. The rattle draws all of our attention. "Um, hold on a second. What about Rhett?"

"What about him?" Dasha asks.

Janice crosses her arms. "Why isn't anyone thinking about his feelings? I know for a fact he wouldn't be happy if he knew Birdie was going to secretly see the first guy she ever kissed. The guy she almost turned him down for. Don't forget that Rhett and Chase are in business together. Going there, behind your boyfriend's back, is just asking for trouble."

I nod, for once agreeing with Janice. "You're right. I definitely don't want to cause trouble between them. A lot is riding on this investment for both of them. Maybe I shouldn't go."

Dasha gives Janice a look. "I don't see how going to talk to him would be a big deal. It's not like they're going on a date."

"A date?" I squeak. "Who said anything about a date?"

My mom holds up a hand. "Birdie, only you can make the decision about what you want to do. The rest of us can have an opinion, but in the end, it's up to you."

I nod, wishing I knew what the right choice was. We sit in silence, mesmerized as the lights twinkle on the tree.

"So how did he look?" Dasha finally asks. "Is he hot?"

"He is very handsome," my mom says with a smirk. "Tall, well-built, great smile. Totally Birdie's type."

"Mom!" I say exasperated, while Dasha squeals with laughter.

"The whole thing is kind of romantic, you have to admit," Dasha says. She loops a garland around her shoulder like a feather boa and spins around dramatically. She lets out a dreamy sigh and flutters her lashes at me.

"Romantic?" Janice says, throwing up her hands. "She's got a boyfriend! Why is everyone forgetting that but me?"

"I'm not forgetting that. I'm just saying it seems like fate—"

I stand up, cutting off whatever Dasha was about to say. My head is starting to spin from all this back and forth. "Okay, enough about Chase. Right now, I just want to forget the whole thing, so let's concentrate on decorating." I raise the volume on the portable speaker pointedly so Christmas carols will drown out their protests.

After a few grumbles, everyone goes back to decking the halls. I try to act normal, but I'm still on edge. Because once my mom put the idea of going to see Chase in my head, I knew I was going to do it.

So at the end of the night, right after I put the star on top of the tree, I Google the schedule for the community college's business classes.

6

———

"Ugh, what are you doing, Birdie?"

It's Monday and the first day back from the Thanksgiving break, and I'm standing in the cold outside of the community college's business wing. I did an embarrassing amount of research to deduce which door Chase would have to come out of, and I hope I'm right.

I blow into my gloves, questioning my sanity in all of this. I probably should have just written him a message on his website, or on any of his businesses' social media channels. What is he going to think when he sees me out here? What if he thinks I'm a total creep?

If he thought that, he wouldn't be wrong. Now that I have his last name, I was able to do a thorough search on the guy, which I'm ashamed to admit, I did at the first opportunity. There wasn't much to find, but I was able to see a few more pictures of him. There was a headshot he took for his business and another one of him on his high school baseball team. I gazed at that one way longer than I should have.

Pacing back and forth, I try to play out different scenarios in my head. It'd be nice if he was happy to see me like he was in the hallway at the Thanksgiving party, but I know that's not likely. Any smiles he had for me then are probably long gone after what I did—

"Birdie?"

I spin around at the sound of my name. Chase is standing behind me, and for a short beat, I drink him in. Seeing him now is no less jarring than it was the first time. And God, he's handsome. No, that's not totally right. Handsome is not the right word. Chase is hot. Like, really hot. The universal type of hot that movie stars and models have. I wonder if he models? My mind conjures a mental image of him shirtless and holding a tray of cupcakes, and my palms start to sweat.

"Birdie? Are you okay?"

I blink, coming back to myself. "Chase. Yes. Hi."

"Hi."

Silence. Shit. He's waiting for me to say something. Of course he is!

Speak, Birdie! Speak!

I suck in a quick and calming breath. "I'm sorry. You're probably wondering what I'm doing here."

"A little," he says, staring at me intently. "Are you here for me?"

"Yes. I came to apologize." I force myself to hold his gaze. "What happened on Thanksgiving ... well, there's a reason why I ... ugh, it's kind of complicated."

A stiff breeze rolls by, throwing strands of hair across my face and making me shiver. The coldness between us isn't helping either. I hate that our two reunions have been so awkward.

"Do you want to go somewhere and get out of the cold?" he asks, seeming to sense my discomfort.

"That'd be great, thank you."

We turn at the same time and start walking toward the parking lot. And to my embarrassment, I find I can't stop peeking at him from the corner of my eye. After thinking about someone for so long then finally seeing them in person, it all feels so surreal.

"There's a café about a mile from here. It's called A Cup of Joy," I say.

"Yup, I know it. I'll meet you there."

I smile up at him. "Okay. Great."

He smiles back, which gives me hope, and then turns and walks to his car.

My eyes rove over his form, unable to stop looking at him. This may be a little dramatic, but he is literal perfection. Even more so because of how casually confident he is. Just as my mind starts to form more mental images of him naked and holding pastries, he turns around and catches me staring.

I jolt, turning quickly and fumbling with my car door handle. Smooth, Birdie. Real smooth. It's nothing short of what I deserve, however. I have a boyfriend, and definitely should not be ogling and having sexual thoughts about another man.

The whole drive over to the café, I force myself to think of the seven elements of photography, in order to keep the inappropriate thoughts at bay.

It works, and when I park my car at A Cup of Joy, I feel ready to tackle this apology and hopefully move on with my life.

Chase is waiting for me at the door, and he smiles and holds it open when I walk up. We settle into a back booth, and I take a moment to enjoy the warm ambiance of the place. A Cup of Joy is my favorite spot because of how cozy it is, especially around the holidays.

It's already decked out for Christmas, with garlands lining the entryways and wreaths on every window. The whole room smells like peppermint, coffee, and just-baked cookies. I inhale, feeling a little burst of holiday spirit.

Chase's soft laugh brings my eyes back to him. "You love it here," he says.

I nod. "Whenever I come in, I feel like I'm transported into someone's living room. I love the homey feel of the place. The chain spots are more convenient, but they don't have this much personality. I'll go out of my way to come here for that very reason."

"Interesting. I'll have to keep that in mind for my shop."

Before I can respond, the waitress comes over to take our order. She eyes Chase a little bit longer than necessary, but he doesn't seem to notice.

"I'll have the Christmas coffee," I tell her when she finally looks over at me.

"That sounds good. So will I," Chase pipes in.

"Two Christmas coffees, coming right up," she says, smiling widely at Chase.

I force back an eyeroll, and once she's out of earshot, I meet his gaze. "You must get that a lot," I say without thinking.

He cocks his head to the side. "Get what?"

"The waitress …" I wave my hand, wishing I never said anything. "Flirting with you."

A slow grin slides across his face. "She was flirting with me?"

"Oh, come on. Don't tell me you didn't notice."

"I didn't. I wasn't paying attention to *her*."

"Oh." The way that he says "her" makes it clear whom he was paying attention to. I look away, because for some reason I feel like I'm trying to walk on thin ice.

The waitress comes back and hands us our coffees. I take a long, deep sip, hoping it will ground me and give me strength to do what I came here to do.

"This is pretty good," Chase says. "I'd add a little brown sugar, but otherwise, good choice."

"Your hot chocolate was way better," I tell him honestly.

He gives me a half-smile. "You don't have to say that."

"But I mean it. Everything I tried on Thanksgiving was truly delicious. You've really got a talent. Your shop is going to take off. I just know it."

He looks happy, but then something in his face changes. "Thanks to Rhett."

The name seems cast a dark spell over the table, and I'm suddenly eager to explain myself. "Chase, he's the reason I'm here. I want to apologize for the other night. For pretending not to know you."

"It's not a big deal."

"To me it is. And if Rhett knew who you were, it would be a big deal to him too."

At this, Chase looks up. "What does that mean?"

I close my eyes, not brave enough to look at him while I explain. "Three years ago, Rhett asked me to be his girl-friend. I told him I had to think about it. And the reason I had to think about it was ... because of you."

My eyes creep open, because something inside me needs to gauge his reaction to my words. He's staring at me with rapt attention, his sharp eyebrows low over his eyes.

I take a breath and forge on. "That kiss we shared, however many years ago, well ... I never forgot it and ... I thought about it and you a lot. I dated here and there before, but Rhett was the first person who wanted to get serious with me. But I just ... couldn't say yes. Not when I was thinking about another guy all the time. So like I told you, I went up to Vermont to look for you. I don't know what I was looking for, or what I thought would happen, but I just had to see if I could find you. It's ridiculous, I know."

I swallow thickly. "Anyway, you and I obviously didn't connect, so when I came back, I said yes to Rhett. But I told him all about you and the kiss. Sometimes I wish I hadn't, because he's never forgotten it. He's asked me more than once what would happen if I ever saw you again. If I would still choose you over him. He's really insecure about it, and I don't blame him. So if he knew that you were *the* Chase from my past, he would have gotten upset that night and it would have ruined everything. That's why I pretended I didn't know you. But I could tell that it bothered you. So I'm sorry for that. I never meant to make you upset."

I chance another look at Chase. There's shock in his eyes, and anger too. But there's something else there that I can't quite put my finger on. Regret, I think, or maybe he's feeling something stronger.

"It's not ridiculous ..." he finally says, his voice soft. "None of it. And I wish I knew you were looking for me, because I wanted to be found. I've thought about you every day since that night."

I bite my lip. "You have?"

"I haven't had a kiss like that since. Have you?"

His question feels like a hammer drop, and a jolt of fear runs through me. Fear, because he's basically confirming that night meant as much to him as it did to me. I didn't imagine the passion between us. We were on the same page back then.

But the thing is, we're not on the same page here today. My gut tells me he's not afraid to raise the stakes, and I'm not prepared for that. There's too much on the line.

I stare back at him, unable to formulate a response.

Everything inside me feels stuck. Because what happens if I do tell him the truth? That he's the only person I ever felt magic with? It would change everything, so I safely chose a different version of the truth.

"No, I haven't had a kiss like that since," I admit quietly. "But I'm with Rhett now, and he's your business partner, and I think it's best if we keep pretending that we've just met."

Disappointment flits across his face. "If that's what you want."

I look down at the table when I respond. "It is."

When I look back up, the look in his eyes makes me feel like he can see right through me. But I'm relieved he's letting me off easy, because I can tell he doesn't want to. After just one night together in the woods, and just one look in his eyes, I know that he's the type who embraces his emotions and isn't afraid to be honest about how he feels. He must be disappointed to realize that I'm not the same way.

"I'd like to be friends," I say.

"Friends it is."

Silence falls over the table, and I quickly try and think of something a friend might ask. "So, are you dating anyone?"

Ugh. Real smooth.

Amusement colors his features. "No, I'm not."

I feel a little relief, but then immediately scold myself for it. "Oh, well, it can be hard moving to an area where you don't know too many people." An idea strikes me, and I suggest it before thinking it through. "Why don't you come to the university this weekend? Rhett's old dorm is throwing a 'Naughty or Nice' party."

He cracks a smile. "What's that?"

"It's just a party. But you can choose to wear a naughty outfit, or a nice one. Like, something sexy or something 'normal.'"

"Interesting. What are you going to wear?"

I look away, feeling my cheeks heat. "I always go with nice. I'm usually the only girl there in a sweater."

His smile grows wider. "I like nice."

I smile too, thinking of how I once told him to go for nice girls.

"So does that mean you'll go?" I ask.

"I don't know." He shrugs and takes another sip of his coffee. "I'm not really one for parties."

"Me either, so I always make an excuse far in advance about why I need to leave early. That's my secret trick."

That makes him laugh. "Well, look at you. Maybe you're a little naughty after all."

"Maybe," I tease.

"I like naughty too."

We share a look, and the hairs on my arm stand on end. What am I doing flirting with him? Conversation between is just so easy. I don't know how to respond to that without sounding borderline inappropriate, so I just laugh lightly and take a sip of my coffee.

"So what's your excuse to leave early this year?" he asks.

"I told Rhett I wanted to see the Christmas Star."

He cocks his head to the side, looking confused. "The Star of Bethlehem? Can't you only see that in late December every, like, eight hundred years or something?"

"Yup, but Rhett doesn't know that. And trust me, he won't look it up, either."

"Hmm, definitely naughty."

I laugh lightly. "So will you come to the party?"

If I'm being honest with myself, I want to see Chase again. I feel a little guilty about that, but maybe the more I'm around him, the less intense it will be between us. Maybe we can eventually get to a place where we actually are friends. Yeah, that should work. A desensitizing plan.

After a beat, he nods. "I'll go."

"Awesome. I'll text you the information."

We exchange numbers, and once I send over the details, we both stand.

"So I guess I'll see you this weekend."

"I guess you will."

We walk to the door in silence and then he walks me to my car. "I'm sorry again," I say. "And thanks for understanding about Rhett."

"You don't have to apologize." He shoves his hands in his pockets. "I get it. And I'll pretend for you, if that's what you want."

I smile. "So what are you going to choose? Naughty or nice?"

He backs away, giving me that curved smile that's been forever etched in my brain. "Birdie, I've never been nice."

7

The next day, my alarm goes off an hour earlier than normal. It's time to focus on taking some photos and finding a perfect submission idea for the holiday contest.

Rhett groans from beside me and throws a pillow over his face. "What the hell, Bird? Shut that thing off."

"Sorry. I'm meeting Dasha. We're going to the Christmas town."

"Why do you have to go at the ass crack of dawn? If you ask me, you're making way too much of this contest. Just go down to the town square and get a nice picture of the tree in the green. Everyone likes that."

I gather my shower stuff, annoyed. "I can't just take any old picture, Rhett. It has to be meaningful."

He looks up, sensing the ire in my tone. "Okay, okay. Sorry. But make sure you're home before dinner, okay? I want to take you to see Chase's shop."

I stop dead in my tracks. "What?"

He rolls over, smiling. "We had the oven delivered the other day, so Chase is going to make some samples. I'd like you to try them. Help me choose stuff for the Christmas party."

See Chase again? So soon? I thought I'd have a few days until the party to reconcile how I'm feeling about the whole thing.

"Birdie?" Rhett says. "Are you okay?"

I shake my head to clear it. "Yeah, sorry. I'm fine. I should be home by then. But I'd better hurry. Dasha will here soon."

He nods and rolls back over, and I hustle into the bathroom. Anxiety fills me as I hurry through my routine. I have no idea why I'm so nervous about seeing Chase again. I was okay yesterday, and set on our plan to be friends. I was going to desensitize myself, and all that.

But the reason I'm so nervous hits me as I'm putting on my makeup. I don't want to be alone with just the two of them. Seeing Chase alone or at a party surrounded by other people is one thing. But alone with my boyfriend as the only witness to the chemistry between us—I don't think I can handle that just yet. What if I give myself away somehow?

So as I walk downstairs to meet Dasha, I text Janice.

Birdie: Are you free later today?

Janice: Depends. What's up?

Birdie: Rhett invited me to Chase's shop to try some samples. Please say you'll come.

Janice: No way. You know I'm gluten-free.

Birdie: Pleeease. I need you there.

Janice: Why? Are you afraid Chase is going to blow your cover or something?

Birdie: No. I know he won't. I ended up seeing him the other day and explained things.

Janice: Oh my God. So you did end up stalking him on campus.

Janice: Did something happen between you guys?

Birdie: I didn't stalk him. And of course nothing happened.

Birdie: We agreed to be friends.

Janice: Friends, huh?

Birdie: Yes. And speaking of, please be a good one and just say you'll come tonight?

Janice: Fine, I'll come. But Chase had better have some low-cal options.

Birdie: You're the best. I'll text you later.

I head downstairs, relieved I'll have a little backup.

Because something tells me I'm going to need it.

8

———

There's a little town outside of New Haven that goes all out for Christmas. Dasha and I call it the "Christmas town" and every year, we do the bulk of our holiday shopping there. We always have a good time, but this year, I'm distracted. Every decoration or storefront is a potential photo op, but I feel like I'm not fully engaging with the sights like I usually do.

We've been here for three hours, and I still don't have any ideas for my project. I thought for sure I'd walk these streets, soak in the holiday spirit, and snap at least three or four possibilities. Dasha has certainly been motivated as she moves from storefront to storefront. But so far, I haven't even lifted my camera. It doesn't make sense. I'm in a Christmas town, yet I'm feeling uninspired.

I think of my dad and how easy it was for him to find inspiration for his paintings. He was always bursting with ideas and finding beauty in the smallest things. My dad especially loved this place. He'd go store to store and buy something in each one, even if it was something he'd never use or want. I used to love those little treasures he'd bring home. One year he bought me a Christmas star necklace for a dollar, and I wore it for years until I lost it.

He made all those purchases because he wanted to give back. He was just like that. My dad was flamboyant and a little self-involved, sure. But deep down, he was a good person. I wish every day I could be more like him.

But maybe I'm just not as imaginative as he was. That thought is depressing, especially because I've lived my entire life trying to live up to his name.

Needing a mental break, I sit down on the nearest bench and place my shopping bags beside me. I'll need to ground myself if I want to gain some perspective. I look up and down the street and force myself to just stop and admire the town's bustling atmosphere. Taking a deep breath, I try to live in the moment without picturing everything through a lens.

Everything here is beautifully decorated. There's garland and twinkle lights wrapped around light poles, bells hanging on every shop door, and old-timey figurines show-cased in every window. A light jingle is playing in the air, and I cock my head to the side to listen.

I really do love this place.

I think of Rhett and the one time I brought him here. We went to Blitzen's—the street's main restaurant and bar, which also happens to be one of my favorite places. He didn't really appreciate it, however, and spent the whole night complaining.

"Who puts whipped cream on a beer?"

*"I would never let my kids sit on **that** Santa's lap."*

"These decorations look worn, like they've been used for years. Can't they afford anything new?"

I never took him there again, but I never stopped coming on my own.

A light snow starts to fall, making me smile. I hold out my glove to catch a flake, thinking of Chase.

The flash of a camera has me looking up. Dasha is standing a few feet away with an ear- to-ear smile. "Okay, not even kidding right now," she says. "But I think I just took my holiday photo."

I laugh out loud. "What? Of me?"

She bends down to pick up two cups of cranberry cider, then hustles over to my side.

"Of course it's of you! It's you on this bench in your cute little coat and hat. Shopping bags beside you. Beautiful street backdrop. Great lighting and a little bit of light snow? Instant winner."

I shake my head. "The theme is supposed to be perfect. I'm far from perfect. Perfectly confused, maybe."

"Still thinking about Chase, huh?"

On the way here, I told her all about our meet-up. Apparently, I really needed to talk to someone who wouldn't judge me, because I ended up talking her ear off.

"Yeah," I admit. "I shouldn't be, but I am."

Her eyes narrow. "Answer me honestly. If you weren't with Rhett, would you want to see where things go with Chase? Because from what you're telling me, I definitely think he would."

"It doesn't matter. I am with Rhett."

"But what if you weren't?"

I sigh, giving her the answer I haven't wanted to admit to myself. "Yes. I would. I felt something with him that night that I haven't felt since."

And I still feel it.

"If you feel that way ... then maybe you should take a break from Rhett. Figure things out. Forever is a long time, and you know that ring is coming."

I immediately shake my head. "No. That would devastate Rhett. And I care about him too much to do that to him."

"But—"

"I can't lose anyone else, Dasha. My dad's death nearly destroyed me. I just ... I can't lose anyone. And I can't be someone else's loss either. Not when I know how it feels."

She gives me a sad smile. "Okay, I know. Maybe you're right. Maybe if you see Chase more often, it will help lessen whatever is going on between you two. I mean, you don't even *really* know him, right? Maybe if you did, you wouldn't feel the way you do now."

I nod, hoping she's right. "Yeah, that's what I'm counting on."

She nudges me with her shoulder. "Now, come on. Let's go see the horses. There may be a holiday photo possibility hiding in the stables."

"Good idea." I adjust the camera around my neck and stand.

"And if you're wondering ..." she starts, looping her arm through mine. "I've still had absolutely no luck on your gift this year, but I'm not giving up hope! I'll find it."

I playfully roll my eyes. Ever since I gave her that camera that one year, she's credited me with giving her her life's purpose. That's why every year since, she's tried to find me the ultimate gift as payback. She's gotten me wonderful things, but for some reason, she's convinced that she hasn't successfully achieved her goal—no matter what I tell her. We go through this every year.

"How about you find me a perfect picture for the contest instead?" I tease.

"Maybe I will," she laughs.

9

______

When I get back to the apartment, Rhett is in the living room, ready to go. He's in a suit, of course. Even for an outing as casual as a visit to a pastry shop, it's Rhett's motto to always conduct business looking your best.

"Oh good, you're home," he says. "Just enough time to change and we'll be on our way."

I look down at my jacket and jeans, then back up at him. "Change? What do you mean?"

"We need to look professional. This is a big deal for me, you know? I want us to look like a power couple."

A power couple? I stare at him, shocked. This is a first. Even when I've visited his dad's offices in the past, he's never made *me* change. "What do you want me to wear? And don't tell me a dress. It's freezing out."

"Please," he says, coming over and grabbing my hands. "I know it's a lot to ask, but it's important. My dad might be dropping by, and I want everything to look official."

A denial is on the tip of my tongue. This is extra, even for him. But when I think of what I'm hiding about Chase, the little bit of guilt eats at me, and I find myself nodding. "Fine."

"Thank you so much, baby. Maybe the little black one?"

I groan, heading for the hallway. "I didn't have any luck with the contest photo, by the way. But thanks for asking."

Rhett's pause speaks volumes. But then I hear footsteps behind me and feel his arms wrap around my waist. "Shit. I'm sorry," he says, nuzzling my neck. "I swear I was going to ask. I've just been distracted with all the planning for the Christmas party."

"It's okay," I sigh. "There's nothing to tell anyway. I took about a hundred pictures, but I already know none of them is good enough."

"Let's look at them together later," he suggests, spinning me in his arms. "You never know—there may be one you forgot about."

I nod, even though I know it will be pointless. But Rhett never offers to look at my photos with me, and a part of me wants to show him my work. "Okay, yeah. Thanks."

"Good. Now go get dressed." He gives me a peck on the lips before heading back to the living room. I turn toward the bedroom, feeling a little bit better.

But my mood sours again when I see the little black dress laid out on our bed. It makes me wonder what would have happened if I refused. Rhett has never once told me what to wear, but that was before this investment. This may be his first deal, but there will be a lot more of them in his future. Is this what I have to look forward to?

Even though I don't want to, I put the dress on and touch up my makeup and hair in record time. There's a pair of heels set out by the door, but I bypass them and grab my booties instead. No way I'm wearing heels in the snow. That's a deal breaker.

When I get back to the living room, Rhett comes over and grabs my hands. I see him glance at my feet, but luckily, he doesn't say anything.

"You look beautiful," he says, kissing me and leading me out the door.

After picking up Janice, we head downtown to a very popular street in New Haven.

"Wow," Janice says to Rhett. "How did you manage this location? He's right next to all the top pizza spots."

Rhett grins as he parallel parks the car. "I know. We got lucky. We've already had some interested customers coming by after dinner to ask if we're open."

He continues to talk about the merits of the location, but my eyes are already on the storefront. It's painted green with a red and white striped awning. The door is large and bright red, reminding me of one you'd find on an old house. There are three small steps leading up to it and gold ornate handrails on either side. I love it immediately, but as I stare at it, I realize something's missing.

"What's the shop called?" I ask, pointing to the blank sign above the awning.

Rhett makes a noise in his throat. "Wish I knew. Chase is dragging his feet on choosing a name. I'm about to just pick one myself."

"You should," Janice says as we all get out of the car. "You obviously have a sense for these things. Besides, you're footing the bill."

Rhett laughs, but stops when his phone rings. He looks at the screen, then holds up a hand. "I have to take this. Be right back."

He walks off and I'm left alone with Janice. She comes over to my side and looks me up and down. "You okay? You look nervous."

"I am, a little," I tell her honestly. "It's just an awkward situation."

She grins. "I, for one, am looking forward to meeting the infamous *Chase*. Seeing the guy who's got my girl's panties in a twist."

"My panties are not in a twist."

She snorts. "If they are, you'd better untwist them quick. Rhett's really going places. This place is guaranteed to be a success with him backing it."

"Chase's pastries may have a bit to do with it too," I say, feeling defensive.

She doesn't respond, because her eyes are locked on something over my shoulder.

"I think someone's waiting for us," she says, grinning like the Cheshire cat.

She loops her arm through mine, and I steel myself before turning around. But it makes no difference. When I lock eyes with Chase, my stomach still bottoms out.

"I think *my* panties are in a twist now," Janice teases. "That man is fine. Like a sexed-up version of Willy Wonka."

I nudge her with my elbow. "Willy Wonka sold candy. Chase sells pastries."

"I don't care what he sells, as long as he wears that apron while doing it."

She's not wrong. I allow myself one moment to fully take him in. He's in dark jeans and a blue Henley, with a white apron that flanks his large body perfectly. His arms are crossed, drawing my gaze to the taut muscles of his biceps. When I finally reach his eyes, that same curved smile on his face makes me blush.

I've been caught staring, and it's not for the first time.

"Hi, Chase," I say, and then clear my throat. "It's good to see you again."

"You too, Birdie."

Janice scoffs. "You guys can drop the act when I'm around, you know." She smiles at Chase. "I know who you are."

Chase raises a brow and looks at me.

I sigh and gesture between them. "Chase, this is my filter-less friend, Janice. And yes, she knows the truth."

"Truth about what?" Rhett says, coming up behind me.

I tense and Janice giggles. "Um ..." I start. "The truth about my sweet tooth."

Rhett grins. "Hate to break it to you, but I think everyone knows the truth about that."

He leans around me and shakes Chase's hand. "Good to see you, man. How's everything going?"

Chase opens the door and holds it aside so we can walk through. "So far, so good. The new oven is the best one I've ever worked with."

"I told you," Rhett says. "That few extra thousand was worth it."

As they talk logistics, I take my first look around the shop. It looks even better than it smells, and that's saying something.

The floors are covered in black and white hexagon-shaped ceramic tiles, and every few feet they form a different design. To the left there's a large display case that runs the length of the shop, and it's not hard to imagine the dark shelves inside it filled with tasty treats. In front of me, there's a wall of white exposed brick covered in empty picture frames, and three small tables are set up in front of it. Off to the right, there's a cozy seating area with a few big chairs that I instantly fall in love with. Apparently, though, I'm the only one.

"I think I was right about these chairs." Rhett sighs as he

eyes the big green seat that I just imagined myself sinking into. "It ages the place. Our product is new and cutting edge. I think we need to keep a modern aesthetic."

"Agreed," Janice says. "They don't match the rest of the place."

"They match the area, though," Chase counters. "There's an old-school vibe on this block. We're next to restaurants that have been open for seventy-five years and they all have spaces like this. I think we should pay tribute to that."

Chase looks at me and smiles.

"Besides," he continues. "I want people to feel comfortable here. To go out of their way to visit the shop instead of a choosing a chain spot."

He echoes the words I used at the coffee shop back to me. I sigh under my breath, feeling a little swept off my feet. "I think the chairs look great. They may not go perfectly with the rest of the furniture, but they work with the tile," I say. "In fact, this place is incredible. You two have done a great job."

"Thanks, babe," Rhett says, grinning. "We're getting there."

He comes over and pecks me on the lips, and over his shoulder I see Chase turn away at the last second, as if he doesn't want to watch. I shouldn't feel guilty, but I do.

Ugh. Operation Desensitize is not going well so far.

"Any ideas on what to do with that empty back room?" Rhett asks.

Chase shrugs. "I figured I'd just use it for storage."

Chase leads us to the empty room in the back of the shop. It's bigger than I thought.

"Maybe you can use it for tastings," I suggest. "Like for weddings and events."

"Great idea," Chase says, smiling. "That way we don't take up room outside—"

"No, no," Rhett says, shaking his head. "We *want* the customers to see the tastings happening. It's good for business."

Chase frowns, but I nod at Rhett. "That's true."

"Now, let's get to the good part," Rhett says, clapping his hands together. "What have you got for us, Chase? And keep in mind, I need the best of the best for the Christmas party. We've got important clients coming."

Chase leads us into the main area, then disappears into another back room. When he comes out, he's got two trays piled with colorful and interesting-looking desserts.

"Do you have anything gluten-free?" Janice asks.

He holds up one tray. "Everything on this tray is gluten-free."

Janice makes a noise in the back of her throat. "Well, it's certainly not calorie-free. You owe me for this, Birdie."

I give her a look. Does she have to be so rude?

I reach out and grab a dish of what looks to be ice cream. "What's this?" I ask.

"Candy-cane ice cream," Chase replies, smiling at me. "I'm still deciding if I should serve it with a candy cane sticking out of it, or if that would be overkill."

I tap my chin. "How about a candy-cane spoon? Might be a little sticky, but I bet the kids would love it."

Chase's eyes light up. "I love that idea. Thanks."

Rhett looks between us. "That's all well and good, but we've already decided on hot ice cream for the party, so we don't need this candy-cane stuff. It'd be weird to have two frozen options in the winter. What else you got?"

For the next half hour, we try over fifteen different desserts, each one better than the last. I'm in awe of

Chase's talent and creativity. He's got the usual desserts, like gingerbread cookies and a yule log, but everything has its own spin. The cookies are made with cinnamon-infused dough, and he made nut crackers with a pudding dip. The fudge is the best I've ever tasted, and the cheesecake—with a pecan graham crust—has my eyes rolling back in my head.

"I can't stop eating," I say, mouth full of trifle. I look to Chase. "These are the best desserts I've ever tasted. Seriously."

Chase smiles boyishly at the compliment, and for a second, I see a shadow of the kid I met in the forest. I swallow thickly and look away.

"Agreed," Janice says, taking one more bite of glazed rum cake. "And you might be surprised to hear this, but I'm not easy to please when it comes to desserts."

Chase and I share a look, and I have to look away before I start laughing.

Rhett reaches down and grabs my hand. "They're right," he said to Chase. "You've outdone yourself. I'll email you a list of what we need for the party." He gets up and looks around, a smug expression on his face. "Just think: without me, you'd still be making this stuff in that cramped basement. And now you're on your way to becoming a real contender in the industry. It's amazing, isn't it?"

In my opinion, the comment is more than a little obnoxious. Chase's face is blank, but I see a hint of derision in his eyes. Luckily, he's saved from replying when Rhett's phone rings again. Rhett's face lights up as he heads for the door. "Be right back."

Once he leaves, Janice stands and looks around. "You have a bathroom? I think I have caramel cookie stuck in my teeth."

"Yeah, through the double doors and to the left," Chase replies.

Once the doors swing shut behind her, the tension in the room seems to compound by the second. Not wanting things to get awkward, I turn to Chase with a smile.

"For what it's worth, I really do love the chairs," I tell him.

"I was hoping you would."

"Oh, yeah?"

He grins. "And I'm hoping you'll help me out with something too."

He walks over to the wall and gestures to the empty picture frames. "I know you're a photographer, so could you please take some photos for me? I'd pay you, of course."

I walk over slowly, stunned by the request. "You want my photos in your shop?"

He gives me a serious look. "Of course. I'd love to have your photos in my shop."

"But you've never seen my work."

"Doesn't matter. They'd be yours."

So much for trying to clear the tension in the room. Every time I'm around Chase, everything just feels ... bigger. More intense.

"That's sweet," I tell him. "I'll help, but on one condition."

"What's that?"

"You don't pay me. I want to do this for free."

He pauses for a moment, and just when I think he's about to argue, he nods. "I'm still brainstorming what to put up here. I was thinking black and white photos of desserts, but I'd like to mix it up with something else."

"Hmm." I pace the wall, eyeing the frames. "I like the dessert idea, and I think the frames above the display case would work for that. But for these frames on the wall, I say you do something a little more unique to who you are. How about some black-and-whites of Vermont?"

Chase blinks, then smiles. "That's perfect."

I nod, gesturing to a big frame in the center. "It'll kind of be an ode to where you started this whole thing, you know? We could take some great scenery shots of places up there that are meaningful to you."

"Like my thinking tree," he says. "That's what I want in the big frame."

My heart pounds. "We can do that."

He smiles, but it doesn't reach his eyes. "I don't know if Rhett will go for it, though. He wanted to showcase pictures of the different technology we use in the kitchens on this wall."

I crinkle my nose. "Like a picture of an oven?"

"Yeah," he sighs. "He and I don't exactly see eye to eye on a lot of things."

"This is your shop," I say. "So you should have the final decision."

"Not when he's footing the bill." He shakes his head, looking away. "And this just can't fail. Because if it does ..."

His words trail off, and I get a weird feeling in my stomach. "If it does ... what?"

"Nothing." He smiles at me again, but it seems forced. "I just want to succeed, that's all."

"You will," I tell him honestly. "And I'll be your most loyal customer."

He looks at me, his eyes full of some unnamed emotion. Watching him watch me has my chest tightening, and I marvel at the fact that he can make me feel this way with just one look. I want to look away, to the cut the invisible cord between us, but I can't.

The bell above the door suddenly jingles and Chase and I both jump.

Rhett comes in, grinning ear to ear.

"What's up?" I ask, trying to sound casual. "You look happy."

"I am, but I'll tell you about it later," he says, throwing his arm around me. "Anyway, we'd better roll out. I'll be in touch, Chase."

Chase nods, his lips thin. "Yeah, okay."

Once Janice comes out, the three of us head to the door and say our goodbyes.

Before I cross the threshold, I look back once more at Chase. He's staring at me too, telling me something with his eyes, but I force myself to look away before I can figure out what it is.

10

—————

"Hold on. Let's get another pic."

This is our fourth picture of the night, but I'm humoring Janice because she's so excited about her outfit for the Naughty and Nice party. She's in a short-skirted Santa costume that doesn't leave much to the imagination. It's not very hard to guess which part of the theme she chose. And I guess the same goes for me, but on the opposite end of the spectrum. I'm wearing my usual—jeans and a white Christmas sweater.

"You know I love you ..." Janice says after she adds the picture to her Instagram story. "But I can't believe you'd choose to wear *that* when you could wear anything."

"It's cold out," I say for what seems like the hundredth time.

"But you could literally wear anything and buy any outfit that you want, whenever you want. I'd do anything to be rich like that. You have the perfect life."

I scoff, feeling weird. "Perfect life? Yeah, right."

"I mean it. You've got the looks. The money. The guy. And you and Dasha are probably going to go on and have really successful businesses as photographers. You have everything."

I put up a hand out to stop her. "If my life was perfect, my dad would be here, for starters."

Her face immediately falls with regret. "You're right. I'm sorry. I'm just in a weird mood, I guess."

"It's all right. I'm in a weird mood too."

"Oh, yeah? Something happen with Rhett?"

I shake my head. "No. But can I tell you something?"

"Uh, yeah. That's what friends are for. What's going on?"

"I invited Chase to the party tonight."

I didn't mean to just blurt it out like that. And maybe I shouldn't have told Janice at all, considering the look on her face.

"You what?"

Cringing, I stop short in the middle of the sidewalk. "After I went to see him at the community college, we went out for coffee—"

"You went on a date? You didn't tell me that!"

"It wasn't a date! It was just too cold to stand outside of his classroom and talk, so we went to the nearest café and that's where we agreed to be friends. He's new to the area and doesn't know a lot of people, so I figured inviting him to the party would be a good idea."

Janice raises a brow. "You're playing with fire, Bird. You need to be honest with yourself, and me. And I know that you're not telling me the whole truth. I mean, this is *me* we're talking about here. I saw the way the way you two looked at each other at his shop, so I know you didn't invite him just because you thought he might be lonely."

"I know." I put my head my head in my hands. "I wanted to see him again, and that's the truth."

"I just don't get it. You have *Rhett*. Why would you be

rocking the boat now? Especially when he's about to ask you to marry him?"

Her tone sets me on edge. "Can you please just not judge me? I'm confused and upset enough as it is, all right?"

"I'll say you are."

The tension that's been popping up between us the past few months comes roaring back. It's happening more and more lately, and I don't know how to fix it or what to do. I make an internal note to talk to her about it later, because we're right outside the party now, so it just doesn't feel like the time to get into it.

"Look, you're right, okay?" I say, putting a hand on her arm. "I am playing with fire, but nothing happened with Chase and nothing is going to happen. I'm with Rhett."

"Okay, I guess I'll have to trust you on that. Because, Bird, I get that Chase is hot. And he's one hell of a chef. But I don't want to see you make a mistake and do something you regret," she says, crossing her arms.

"I'm not going to do anything. Don't worry. In fact, I was thinking the more I see him, the better. The shock value might wear off, you know?"

She gives me a look. "Whatever you say. Let's just go inside. You ready?"

Her tone is light, but her shoulders are still rigid, so I put down my bag and grab the edge of my sweater. I was going to wait to do this, because I really don't want to start the night on a bad note.

"Almost," I say, whipping the material over my head.

When she sees my white studded corset, her jaw drops.

"Okay, now I'm ready," I grin.

Surprising her early was the right move, because her face breaks out into a wide smile and she throws her hands in the air. "Holy shit! Now that's what I'm talking about."

"Can't be the nice girl all the time," I giggle. I reach down into my bag to grab a pair of heels, and Janice helps steady me so I can put them on.

"Rhett is going to die when he sees you in that," she comments as we walk into the party.

A shameful little voice inside me responds that maybe I didn't wear this outfit for Rhett, but I stamp that out quickly. I don't want to believe I'd do something so wrong.

But Janice is right. When we find Rhett in the kitchen a few minutes later, it's obvious my outfit choice has shocked him to his toes.

"*Whaaaat*," he says, putting down his drink and walking toward me. "You never choose naughty."

"I figured since it's our last year, I'd switch things up."

"Mm, well, I'm glad you did. You look hot, babe."

"Thank you. So do you."

Rhett always chooses naughty, and wears the same outfit every year. Well, if you can call shirtless and a pair of slacks an outfit. This year, however, he's paired it with suspenders and a Santa hat.

He leans down and pecks my lips gently. "This party just keeps getting better and better. You'll never guess who's here."

"Try her," Janice drawls.

I glare at her then turn back to Rhett. "Who?"

"Chase! My client."

"What a coincidence," Janice says, tapping her chin. "How would he know about this very private party at a college he doesn't even go to?"

The look I give her could start a literal fire.

"He's here?" I try to keep my tone casual, but even to me, it sounds shaky.

"Yeah, some girl invited him but then didn't show. What

a bitch, huh? I told him there'd be tons of girls here for him to choose from instead." His eyes swing to Janice. "Hey, what did you think of him the other day, Jan? He's a nice guy. Maybe you could show him a good time."

Jealousy flares green and nasty in my gut.

Janice and Chase? No way.

Janice takes one look at my face and rolls her eyes. "Sorry, not in the market for the ice cream man," she says, waving Rhett off. "But thanks, anyway."

Rhett laughs loudly, but her joke annoys me. She's really on a roll tonight, and I make it a point to add all this to the list of things I want to talk to her about.

"Hey, there he is," Rhett says, waving a hand over his head. "Chase, over here!"

Rhett says it like a command, and when I turn around and see the look on Chase's face, it's obvious he took it like one. His lips are pressed together, and from his tight body language, it's clear he's irritated. But then he sees me and everything changes.

Rhett called me hot when he saw me, but the way Chase looks at me makes me feel it. His eyes slowly sweep over me, as if he's memorizing every inch of my body. Our eyes meet for just a moment, and there's no mistaking the desire in his gaze. He isn't even trying to hide it. Right before he looks away, one corner of his lips turns up, and I know he's thinking of our conversation at the coffee shop about naughty versus nice.

"What's up?" he finally says, looking back at Rhett.

Rhett pauses, then wraps a hand around my waist and pulls me close. "Just telling the girls you got stood up."

Chase smiles, then looks at me. "Something like that."

"No offense, but that sweater could have something to do with it." Rhett chuckles. "If you want to find a new girl for the night, I'd show some skin. The naughty ones always get laid around here."

Ugh. I hate it when Rhett says immature things like that. His arm around me suddenly feels like a heavy weight.

Chase raises a brow. "You need to take your shirt off to get women, Rhett?"

"No need for me to get women," Rhett quips. "Not when I've got the best one right here."

The sentiment is sweet, and it should make me happy. But instead, it's awkward. I avoid Chase's eyes, but next thing I know, he's whipping off his shirt and drawing my gaze back to him.

Janice makes a small, approving sound, and I don't blame her. Chase is ripped. Not like bodybuilder ripped, but like Chris Evans ripped when he came out of that transformation machine in *Captain America*. A few girls around us stop and stare, and I can feel Rhett tense beside me, which isn't surprising. He always likes to be the center of attention, and while Rhett is fit, he's nowhere near Chase's level.

"You're right," Chase says to Rhett, his voice light. "If I want a girl like Birdie, maybe I should pull out the big guns."

Rhett nods, but I can sense he's irritated. "Let's play a game," he suddenly says. "King's Cup."

Great. Rhett is obviously feeling competitive and now wants to one-up Chase by beating him at some dumb drinking game.

It's going to be a long night.

11

───────

"Okay, so does everyone know the rules?" Rhett asks, fanning out a deck of cards in the middle of the table.

"You need to remind me," Chase says. "I haven't played King's Cup since high school."

The barb is obvious, and I give Chase a look. The last thing I want is for him to stoop to Rhett's level of competitiveness.

All the heated looks he's giving me aren't helping either, no matter how they make me feel. That type of thing can't be happening between us. Especially not when I'm doing my best to act normal and play the part we agreed to. It would make things a lot easier if he would do the same.

Luckily, Rhett doesn't seem to realize Chase's words were somewhat of a veiled insult.

"All work and no play for you, huh, Chase?" Rhett says, grinning. "Janice, you want to do the honors while I grab the beer?"

"Sure," Janice smiles at him, then turns to Chase. "Each player takes a turn picking a card. Each card has a different activity or action assigned to it. Two is you so you'd drink, three is me so I'd drink, et cetera, et cetera. It's easy to catch on."

"Ah, that's right. All coming back now," Chase says.

He winks at me just as Rhett slams a beer down in the center of the table.

"Then let's play," he says. "Chase, you're our honored guest. You can go first."

Chase pauses for a beat, then draws a card. "Six."

"Dicks," Rhett says. "That means the boys drink. Cheers, Chase."

Chase taps his beer against Rhett's, then they both drink. Afterward, when no one else at the table is looking, Chase sends me a "this is the stupidest thing I've ever played" sort of look, making me smile.

"My turn," Janice says, drawing a card. "Eight."

"Pick a mate," Rhett says. "They'll have to drink every time you do."

"Then I pick you," Janice replies with a grin. "You seem down to drink double tonight."

"Always," Rhett says on a laugh. They both drink and then it's Rhett's turn. "Two," he says, spinning the card in his fingers. "That means you. So I pick someone to drink."

I know he's going to pick me before he says it, so I'm not surprised when his hand points in my direction. "I choose Birdie. She's a little bit more fun when she's drunk, if you know what I mean."

My cheeks heat with embarrassment and shock. Looks like Rhett's already drunk, because he'd never say something like that sober. He turns into such an ass when he's had too much "Ha. Ha. Very funny," I tell him, trying to play off how embarrassed I am.

"I'm just teasing, baby," Rhett says, leaning over and

pressing a sloppy kiss to my cheek. I let him do it, even though I want to pull away.

It's my turn, so I draw a card. "Three. That means me, so I guess I drink again." Thank God I got something easy.

Chase also picks a three, and then Janice picks another two and gives the drink to Chase. Rhett gets a ten and I groan under my breath. Categories. The person who draws the card picks a category, and then you go around the table naming things that fit into that category. Whoever can't think of one on their turn loses. Rhett always picks the same category when he draws this card.

"I choose sex positions," Rhett says, waggling his brows. "And I'll kick things off with boring old missionary. Just to get it out of the way."

"Doggy style," I say when it's my turn.

"Ohh, your favorite," Rhett drawls.

This time anger comes along with the embarrassment. I turn to him, wanting to say something, but when I try to get the words out, they get stuck in my throat. Like always, I freeze.

"Cowgirl," Chase says when it's his turn. His voice sounds tight, and when I look up at him, he's glaring at Rhett. A small stab of guilt runs through me since technically, I was the one who put yet another obstacle between them.

"Reverse cowgirl," Janice hollers, swinging a lasso above her head.

"Wheelbarrow," Rhett says next.

"Sixty-nine," I add.

"Rock n' roll," Chase says.

Rhett slaps his knee. "Dude, come on, you made that up. You drink."

At first it seems like Chase is going to fight it, but instead he just picks up his beer and takes a sip. He meets my eyes over the can, and something in my body sparks red hot. I have a feeling he didn't make it up, and my mind starts racing thinking of what the rock n' roll position could be. I eventually force my eyes away, wishing I could do the same with my attraction to him.

The game continues on pretty uneventfully until Janice gets a Jack. Jack is the game Never Have I Ever, and the mischievous look she's sending me is making me nervous.

We each hold up a hand of five as she starts. "Never have I ever … kissed a girl."

Chase and Rhett both put a finger down. I sense Chase's eyes on me but I refuse to look in his direction. Ugh, this is so awkward.

"Never have I ever kissed a guy," Rhett shoots back.

Janice and I both lower a finger.

"Never have I ever been skydiving," I say, hoping to get the conversation away from kissing and on to anything else.

No one puts a finger down, and then Chase goes.

"Never have I ever been to California," he says.

I shoot him a grateful smile, happy that he took my lead about steering the conversation. But unfortunately Janice is next, and she's clearly out to get me tonight.

"Never have I ever …" she starts, eyes narrowing on me. "Thought about having sex with the first person I ever kissed."

I suck in a breath. I cannot believe she just said that. The comment is so pointed and weird that even Rhett is momentarily thrown for a loop. One thing I know for sure is that I don't want to respond to this one. Not with Chase sitting right there. Thinking on my feet, I casually reach out and tip my beer, spilling it onto my lap.

"Oh, geez," I groan, pushing back my chair. "I'm such a klutz."

"Damn, babe," Rhett says with a grin. "You must be drunker than I thought."

"Isn't that your first beer?" Janice asks cattily.

I stare at her, overwhelmed and hurt by her behavior. And after a beat, her face falls and I see a flash of regret. Yeah, well, it's too late for that.

Chase reaches out to me as if he wants to help, but I've had enough. Enough of Rhett's embarrassing jokes, enough of Janice's passive-aggressive teasing, and way more than enough of whatever this tension is between Chase and me. It's all too much.

"I'll be right back," I say to the table, and without waiting for a response, I turn and walk away.

Desperate for air, I beeline for the back door. And once I get to the backyard, I head directly for the side of the house. There's a tree there that I always used as a spot to get some space, back when Rhett lived here. Unfortunately, it was cut down last year, and all that's left is a stump. I sit on it, wrapping my arms around myself. I should have brought my jacket. But I don't want to go back inside to get it. I'm not in the mood to party. I'm not in the mood to do anything, really. Everything just feels so wrong lately. Since Chase has come back into my life, everything is upside down.

The crackle of leaves has me looking up, and seconds later, Chase emerges from the shadows. He has his jacket in his hands.

"Take this. It's freezing."

"I'm okay."

"You've got half of a shirt on and a lap full of beer. Take it."

After a beat, I slowly grab the jacket from his hand.

"Thanks." I put it on, trying not to revel in both the delicious heat and the woodsy smell of it. "What are you doing out here?"

"I came to see if you were okay."

I look up at him. "Is that really why you're out here, Chase?"

"What's that supposed to mean?"

I open my mouth to speak, but the words freeze in my throat, so I just shake my head.

"No, tell me what that means," he pushes.

"It doesn't mean anything."

"Birdie, talk to me."

His voice is gentle but firm. He's not going to let me get away with not telling him, so I stand up, needing to look him in the eye for this. For some reason, when I'm looking at him, the words flow freely.

"You know exactly what I mean. All the looks you're giving me. All the shade you're throwing at Rhett. It's not right. I have a boyfriend, Chase."

"Yeah, a shitty one."

My jaw drops. "You don't even know him. You don't even know me, for that matter."

"I know enough. Why are you with him?"

"That's none of your business."

"Maybe not. But I'm asking you anyway."

I narrow my eyes. "If you hate him so much, why are you working with him?"

"Because I have no choice."

The sudden vulnerability in his voice gives me pause. There's something there in his eyes, but then it passes and I think of his comment the other day at the shop. He said he needed to succeed, but why? Maybe there's something more to it than just the triumph of a dream come true.

"So tell me," he continues. "Why are you with him?"

I look away, unable to take the intensity in his eyes anymore, and then I give his question some real thought. I'm with Rhett for a lot of reasons. He's a good guy, albeit a little immature. He's smart and motivated, and at times can be really sweet. He's condescending and a little self-centered, but everyone has flaws. I don't tell Chase any of these things, though. But I do tell him the main reason, which keeps resounding in my head. "Because I know what it feels like to be abandoned, and I can't do that to someone who loves me."

Chase stares at me for long seconds. "That's not a good reason, Birdie."

"It's good enough for me."

His nostrils flare, but he doesn't respond. He just stares at me, devouring me with his sharp stare.

I throw up a hand. "See, this is what I mean. You can't look at me like that."

"I can't help the way I look at you. I feel like I'm starved for you. I've wanted to look at you every single day since the night you walked away from me."

His words send some unnamed emotion rolling down my spine. I bring my eyes to his and drop my voice down to a whisper. "You have to cool it with this intensity. I can't handle it."

"It's not intensity."

"Then what is it?"

He raises both eyebrows. "Chemistry. In its purest form. That's what you're feeling. I'm feeling it too. But the difference is I'm not trying to run away from it."

I shake my head, not wanting to believe that it's true. "It can't be. We don't even know each other."

"I may not know your birthday or your favorite movie,

but I know what you look like when you're scared. I know what you sound like when you feel all hope is lost. I know what your hair smells like when it blows across my face." His jaw flexes and his eyes drop to my lips. "And I still remember what you taste like, even after all these years ..."

My whole body seems to lift briefly off the ground, powered by my pounding heart.

"Birdie, please. I get that you think you have to play some kind of role when you're in front of him, but don't pretend when it's just us. Tell me how what you're feeling."

I open my mouth to respond, even though I have no idea what I want to say. But then Rhett calls my name, and it breaks the spell between us, popping the ever-present bubble of magic.

I take off the coat and hand it back to him. Then, backing away, I give him the two words that are blaring on repeat in my head. "I can't."

I walk back over to Rhett, praying I don't look as emotional as I feel. He's standing by the back door, and when he sees me he saunters over, a big smirk on his face.

"What are you doing out here?" he asks. "I thought you were going to get cleaned up."

"I changed my mind," I say, rubbing my arms. "And I needed a break from the game."

"Come on. It was just getting good. Come back in and play."

He reaches out to grab my arm but I push him away. "No," I snap. "I'm not playing anymore. You really embarrassed me back there."

"What? How?"

I open my mouth to tell him, but the words don't come. If he doesn't know what he said wrong, then what's the point of telling him?

"Nothing, never mind," I say, pushing past him. "I'll see you at home."

"What? You're leaving?" he says, following behind me. "Whatever I did, I'm sorry. Please, just stay."

I shake my head, turning around to face him. "I already told you I was going to see the Christmas star. So I'll see you at home, okay?"

"Birdie, wait—"

I yank open the door and walk back inside before he can try to stop me again. I need space and time from both Rhett and Chase. After grabbing my coat, I head for the door, wondering how the hell I got myself into this mess.

wake up the next morning to a crash. Gasping, I pop up in bed and throw the covers off.

Whatever it was came from the living room, so I hustle down the hallway as fast as I can. Rhett got home late last night and he was pretty drunk. He passed out on the couch, which was fine by me, because I was not in the mood for a confrontation. But now I'm wondering if he was *too* drunk and has somehow hurt himself.

"Rhett? Are you okay?"

I hear a garbled sound, and I round the corner just in time to see his head pop out of from a pile of boxes. "I'm fine," he says, breathing heavily. "I didn't mean to wake you."

"What's all this?" I ask, gesturing around the living room. The entire floor is covered in boxes and colorful string lights, and in the corner of the room there's a massive pine tree.

He pulls himself up and dusts off his pants before walking over to me. "I went out this morning to get us decorations. I wanted it to be a surprise."

"But you hate the smell of pine. And the lights give you a headache."

It's one of the reasons why we have minimal decorations every year, and why I still go over and help my mother. Decorating is a major tradition for me, and it was a huge bummer when I found out in the beginning that Rhett wasn't a fan. So this whole thing is very, very confusing.

"But you love it," he says, pulling me into his arms. "And I was a drunk asshole last night. So consider this an apology."

I raise a brow. "So you remember what you said, then?"

"Yes, and I'm sorry," he says, very deliberately, before leaning down and kissing my nose. "The sexual comments were out of line. I guess I just can't help bragging about you once in a while."

"Those are the wrong things to brag about," I say. "And it wasn't funny."

"I know it wasn't. I don't have any excuse, but it won't happen again."

I'm not sure if I want to, but eventually I wrap my arms around his waist and shoot him a half smile. "I hope not."

He smiles, then leans down to kiss my lips. "Now, help me untangle these damn lights before I throw them off the balcony."

I giggle, picking up the heap and walking over to the couch to get started. This was really, really sweet of Rhett, and my mood has picked up considerably. Almost enough to make me forget about my conversation with Chase last night. But despite how I feel, maybe it was a conversation worth having. Chase needs to know where I stand, and that I'm with Rhett. Rhett, who went out of his way to do something nice for me this morning.

Smiling, I look up at him but immediately frown. He's standing by the TV, watching a college hockey game.

"We're supposed to be decorating," I say, exasperated. "Can we give the sports a rest for once?"

"Sorry," he says, eyes still on the TV. "University up north has got this stud freshman named Theo Armstrong. He's the best I've seen a while. He'll be picked up by the pros in no time."

I raise a brow. "Put on a Christmas movie. Or at least some music. Come on. This was your idea."

He sighs, but then he shuts off the TV and grabs his phone. Seconds later, "Grandma Got Run Over by a Reindeer" starts playing, making me laugh.

"I hate Christmas music," Rhett says. He goes over to the corner and starts putting the tree in its stand, then turns to me with a smile. "But we can play it all morning and well into the night if that will make you happy. That's how much I love you."

My heart softens, and it definitely helps lessen the blow of the embarrassment yesterday. This is a really thoughtful apology, but a part of me wishes that I hadn't caved so easily. He really humiliated me last night. But relationships are about forgiveness and compromise. And if Rhett is doing all of this for me, then the least I can do is try to forget about yesterday.

"I love you too," I finally respond.

He smiles, then turns back to the tree. "Anyway, wasn't it so random Chase was at the party last night? Definitely the last person I was expecting to see. But I guess it makes sense."

My body tenses, and I keep my eyes on the lights. "Why does it make sense?"

He shrugs. "He's a moody bastard, but he's a decent-looking dude. Not surprising he found a girl so quick."

I don't know how to respond to that, so I busy myself with opening up a few ornament boxes.

"What do you think of him?" Rhett asks suddenly.

My cheeks flush pink, and I make sure not to look over at him. "Umm ... he seems nice. Obviously very talented. His desserts are amazing."

Rhett scoffs. "He's lucky he is talented. I wouldn't be dealing with him otherwise."

Something in his tone doesn't sound right, so I turn around to gauge his expression. Sure enough, he's got the half-pout, half-angry look on his face that he gets when he's annoyed. "What do you mean by that?" I ask.

Rhett shrugs. "I just didn't like the way he was showing off last night. Did you see him take off his shirt?"

I bark out a laugh. "You told him to!"

"I know. But he was so smug about it. I get the vibe he kind of thinks he's better than everyone else. But I don't know why he'd think that. He wouldn't even have a shop if it weren't for me."

Bursts of anger pop in my stomach, and I open my mouth before I think better of it. "I'm pretty sure he knows that, Rhett. From what I've seen he's been nothing but grateful. He's quiet, sure, but that doesn't mean he's arrogant."

Rhett turns to me, scanning my face. It looks like he's about to say something, but then his shoulders sag. "You're right. I'm being a Grinch. I don't want to ruin things. Especially on our anniversary."

I cock my head to the side. "Huh? Our anniversary is in January."

He comes over to me, pulling me into his arms. "Yes, but today is the day we met. Don't you remember?"

"Janice's Christmas party," I sigh. "And of course I remember. You had on that horrible red and green sweater."

His jaw drops in mock offense. "Excuse you, but that was a Givenchy."

"Goes to show you money can't buy taste."

He laughs, throwing his head back. "Okay, I get it. The sweater was a bit extra. But you fell in love with me anyway."

"You didn't give me much choice. You followed me around half the night until I agreed to a date," I tease.

"That's because you were, and still are, the most beautiful woman I've ever seen."

He leans down and presses a kiss against my lips, and I soften. "Thanks, Rhett."

"It's true," he says, pulling away and heading back to the tree. "Seeing you that night completely changed my plans."

I pull out the tree skirt and shake it out. "Speaking of random," I say. "It was weird you were at Janice's party when you didn't even know her."

Rhett is in the corner and I can't see his face. "I told you. A friend invited me."

"And then bailed," I say, thinking of what he told me that night. "Just like what happened with Chase. That's why I don't think it was weird that he was there last night."

"You're right," Rhett says, popping his head around the branches. "Now, bring those lights over. Let's get this done before I'm completely covered in sap."

13

———

*J*anice: I'm sorry! Please stop ignoring me

My thumbs hover over the keypad, but at the last moment, I close the text and put my phone in my bag. Dasha gives me a knowing look from the desk beside me. "Janice again?"

"Yeah."

Dasha sighs. "You've been ignoring her for over a week. You're going to have to respond to her sometime."

"I know. I'm just not ready."

"I get it. She was way out of line. But ..."

My head snaps to her. "But what? Don't tell me you're on her side."

"Of course not." She holds up two hands. "I was just going to say that she's right when she says you're playing with fire."

Thinking of Chase, my pulse quickens. "Maybe. But after the conversation we had, I don't think I'll be seeing him again. I kind of shut things down."

I haven't heard from Chase in a week either. Not that I was expecting to, but it's still a little weird after seeing him three times in one week. And I wish I could say out of sight, out of mind, but unfortunately that hasn't been the case.

"If you want to be with Rhett," Dasha says. "Then that was the right move."

"Right."

But if it's really the right move, then why do I feel so shitty about it? I sigh, rubbing a hand down my face, tired of the moral back-and-forth of it all.

"Anyway, Donovan will be over soon," I say to her. "Show me what you've got."

Dasha's face lights up and she hands me an envelope. When I open it and see what's inside, I break into a smile. It's the photo of me sitting on the bench in Christmas town. "It's my picture."

"Yup, I'm going to submit it this weekend. After I play around with the lighting effects a bit and get Donovan's advice."

My eyes go wide. "This weekend?! But that's so early. What if you take another great photo in the meantime?"

The situation is totally possible. Dasha is an amazing photographer, and may be the only person I know who likes taking pictures more than I do. I fell in love with photography because I like to live in singular moments, even after they pass. But Dasha loves the bones of photography, and the technique required to make each piece of the photo a work of art. She'll work for hours to get everything just right, and she usually reaches that goal—or, at least, she does in my opinion. She's definitely a contender to win this year's holiday contest. And even though she's major competition for me, I couldn't be prouder.

"Even if I do take other pictures, none of them will be better than this one," she responds. "To me, this is perfect."

I look up and into her eyes. "It's a beautiful picture,

Dasha. Congratulations. And it means a lot that your perfect picture features me."

"Thank you." She smiles. "Now show me what you've got."

My shoulders droop. "Nothing good." I hand her over a few photos I took of the horses in Christmas town, and a couple of others that I shot of some snow outside my apartment.

Her lips purse as she flips through. "These are good, but yeah, nothing that feels right for the contest. You'll get there. Don't worry."

I appreciate her honesty and her support. All my confidence seems to have gone out the window, and I don't have much hope I'll find something in time.

Professor Donovan comes over and smiles at Dasha. "What's this I hear that you already have your submission?"

"I have Birdie to thank," Dasha says, turning to me. "She just happened to be in the right place at the perfect time."

"Can I see it?" he asks. "Or would you prefer to keep it private?"

"I'd actually love for you to take a look," Dasha replies. "And please, be brutally honest. I don't know if I want to submit it as a black-and-white photograph, or if I should go for a more of wintry palette."

Professor Donovan takes the envelope and pulls out the picture. He scans it for a few long moments, then brightens. "Dasha, you've outdone yourself. This picture invokes the spirit of Christmas, but also, thanks to Birdie here, it highlights a central image of realism. See me after class and we can talk about lighting."

"Okay, thank you," Dasha says, smiling widely.

I'm happy for her. I swear I am. But I'd be happier if I actually had something better than a few horses for my subject matter. Professor Donovan takes one look at my expression, then points across the room.

"Dasha, are you opposed to showing this photograph to Edward? His pieces are all very dark and one-dimensional, and he needs to see a picture that showcases a bit more duality."

"Sure," she says, grabbing her envelope. With one more smile at me, she walks away.

"And how about you, Birdie? Do you mind showing me what you've got for the contest?"

"I would if I had something," I say a bit grumpily. "I guess I was counting on the parameters to guide me. I just can't wrap my head around the word 'perfect.'"

"You're not alone there. Trying to find perfection seems fruitless, and I think that's the whole point. Let's start from the beginning. What does Christmas mean to you?"

"It means ..."

What does it mean? It's means Santa Claus and my mom smiling while handing out hot cocoa to the family. It means my dad and his bright red bathrobe making maple syrup pancakes at five a.m. It means singing holiday songs with Dasha and watching the same movies a hundred times. It means looking out the window, wishing my dad were still here, and believing in miracles. It means ... Chase at midnight.

I swallow that last thought and say, "It means my dad and magic and ..."

And Chase. His name keeps resurfacing in my head. I don't want to say anything about him to Professor Donovan, however. That would be weird; and besides, he wouldn't understand. Chase isn't just some guy I'm attracted to. He's the person who gave me hope in a single night. Hell, he gave me a whole new way of coping. After that Christmas, things were different for me.

"I suppose memories," I finally say.

The corner of his lip quirks up. "Magic, hm?"

"Yeah." I smile. "When my dad was alive, we'd book the same cabin in Vermont every Christmas. Mistletoe Cabin, it was called. My dad loved it there. He used to say there was magic in the woods around it. I'd stay up late and look out the window, imagining I was seeing all sorts of different things. I believed it was all real back then."

"Sounds to me like for you, Christmas is in Vermont."

I look away. "It used to be."

He taps the desk in front of me with one finger. "Your dad, magic, and memories. Those themes feel pretty close to perfect. I'd take a picture that encompasses all three of those things. Think about how and where you can find that." Then, with a knowing smile, he walks away.

Seconds later, I feel like I've been struck by a lightning bolt.

I have to go back to Vermont. That's where my perfect picture is waiting and ready to be found. It's the only place where I can find my dad, magic, memories—and yes, even Chase.

Excited, I take out my phone and pull up Mistletoe Cabin on a rental site. It's just as beautiful as I remember, and the sight of it brings forward a rush of happy anticipation.

It's already booked for this coming weekend, but I'm able to snag it for Sunday and Monday, and Tuesday night. I'll have to skip a few classes to squeeze in this trip, but it will definitely be worth it.

And just like that, I'm rejuvenated and enthusiastic

about the contest like I haven't been since before it was announced. I only wish I thought of this earlier.

By the end of class, I'm in a great mood. That mood quickly sours, however, when I spot Janice in the hallway after class, waiting for me.

Dasha nudges me with her elbow. "Do you want me to stay?" she asks quietly.

"No, it's okay."

"All right. I have to go anyway. I think I finally have a lead on your perfect gift."

I give her one last smile, then turn to Janice.

"I'm sorry," she says once our eyes meet.

She looks sorry. But for some reason, I don't want to forgive her. What she did was mean and uncalled for, and had the potential to really cause a big mess. What was she even thinking, doing what she did at the party?

I stare at her, wanting to rant and rave and tell her exactly how I feel inside.

But as always, I back down, because not forgiving her would take too much of my energy. I let my feelings go with a heavy sigh. "It's okay. But why would you do that when you knew how weird this situation has been for me?"

"I don't know. I know this isn't an excuse but I've just been really stressed out lately. I guess I was just having a little fun or was trying to make a joke or something and it got out of hand. I promise I won't do anything like that ever again. Now, pretty please, say that you'll forgive me?"

She comically bats her eyelashes and it strikes me that she knows I'll forgive her, because I always do. It's not right. Has Janice always been like this and I just never noticed? Anger has me clenching my fists, and the emotions rising inside me are getting stronger and harder to tamp down. But even still, I don't have the guts to tell her how I really feel.

"I forgive you."

She smiles and pulls me into a hug. "Thank you. Now that that's out of the way, want to go gown shopping this weekend for Rhett's Christmas party? I'm thinking we can hit up the outlets and then the mall."

"I can't," I say. "Something came up. But maybe next weekend?"

"Fiiine," she says, checking her phone. "Better sales around then anyway, not that you need them. Anyway, gotta roll. Later, babe."

I watch her walk away before heading out to the parking lot. I'm thankful she didn't ask about my plans, because I don't want to tell her about Vermont. I don't want to tell anyone for that matter. Because while I have high hopes that I will find a picture—what if I fail? I'd rather not build up anyone else's expectations, just in case I have to let them down along with myself.

When I get to my car, I'm surprised to find a white box sitting on the hood. It's tied with a white, red, and green ribbon, and there's a tag that reads *Holiday Moose*.

My heart skips a beat. It's from Chase. I open the box and, sure enough, there are three containers of his infamous chocolate mousse. Smiling, I grab the note wedged in beside the containers. "If *you can't* ... then can we at least try to be friends?"

14

———

For the rest of the night, I can't get Chase's note out of my mind.

I don't know what to do. I want to be friends with Chase, but I can't deny a part of me was relieved when I walked away. Being around him is so confusing, and I don't think I'm strong enough to handle the way he makes me feel.

I told him *"I can't"* and I meant it.

Rhett snores beside me, reminding me exactly why *I can't*. I won't just abandon Rhett because Chase came back into my life unexpectedly. I can't give in to how I feel because something new and shiny has come along.

But maybe I gave up too easily on my original plan for how I'd handle the Chase situation.

I've only seen him a few times. We've barely had time to get used to each other. Maybe I should think about reviving my desensitization idea. It wasn't a bad plan. Maybe I just need to give it a chance to actually work.

Making a quick decision, I pull up his contact number and open a text.

Birdie: Yes, I'd like to be friends.

I send it, then sink down into the blankets, feeling anxious. I peek over at Rhett again, but he's sound asleep. I feel a little guilty, but I'm not doing anything wrong. I'm doing this for Rhett's benefit too. Chase is his client, and it's only right that I get along with Rhett's clients. Besides, I told Chase I could only be friends with him. I'm doing the right thing.

Seconds tick by, and just when I'm about to put my phone away, a text pops up.

Chase: I was starting to worry someone stole that box.

Birdie: If they knew what was inside, someone would have.

Birdie: That mousse was delicious.

Chase: *Moose.

Birdie: Not to be confused with reindeer ;).

Chase: Ha. Ha.

Chase: So ... friends?

Birdie: If the offer still stands ...

Chase: I'm willing to try.

Chase: I'll be a better friend to you than Janice, that's for sure.

Birdie: You noticed, huh?

Chase: She wasn't exactly subtle.

Chase: She reminded me of Harper.

Birdie: Who's Harper?

Chase: My ex-girlfriend. The one who told me I was a bad kisser.

Birdie: Ah, the mean girl.

Chase: You were right, you know.

Chase: I've stayed far, far away from girls like Harper and Janice since then.

Birdie: Janice isn't normally like that.

Birdie: And she apologized today.

Chase: I hope she deserves to be forgiven.

I don't know if she does, but I don't want to tell him that. Something about the way he says things pushes me out of my comfort zone, and while it might help to explore my feelings about Janice, I can't create that kind of additional bond between Chase and me. So I change the subject.

Birdie: So are you saying you've only dated nice girls?

Chase: You're interested in my love life, huh?

Birdie: You're the one who brought it up.

Chase: That's a conversation for another day.

Birdie: Okay, Mr. Secretive. Not very *friend*ly of you.

Chase: Lol, okay. What do you want to know?

Chase: But wait, if you ask me a question, then I get to ask one too.

Birdie: Tell me about your last girlfriend.

Chase: I already did.

Birdie: You haven't had a girlfriend since Harper?!

Chase: She kind of did a number on me.

I stare at my phone, shocked. A guy like him has never had a serious girlfriend? How is that possible? He's such a catch.

Birdie: You? Single all these years? I don't buy it.

Chase: It's the truth.

Chase: And now it's my turn to ask something ...

Anxiety seizes in my chest. I really hope he doesn't bring up Rhett. But then he surprises me in the best way.

Chase: When is your birthday?

Birdie: Lol. January 2nd

Chase: Should have known you were a winter baby.

Birdie: I bet you are too.

Chase: December 25th.

Birdie: Oh my God! Christmas.

Birdie: Wait, Harper dumped you the day before your birthday?!

Chase: Told you she did a number on me.

Birdie: I should go up there and give her a piece of my mind.

Chase: I'm actually going to Vermont this weekend.

Chase: Have a few things I need to take care of.

Holy shit. He's going to Vermont this weekend? What are the odds? I debate whether it would be wise to tell him that I'll be there too, but the coincidence is too weird to ignore.

Birdie: I'm actually going up on Sunday.

Birdie: Spending a few days at Mistletoe.

A few minutes tick by before he responds.

Chase: I could always push my trip back a couple of days if you wanted to drive together.

I sink further into the covers, my mind racing. Drive to Vermont with Chase? With all that time alone together in a car? I don't think I can do it. But ... I did just tell him I wanted to be friends. And maybe that time together will give me the exposure therapy I need.

I look over at Rhett, guilt creeping back in. But I'm really not doing anything wrong. It's just two friends sharing a car together. But still ...

Chase: It would be a good time for us to take those pictures for the shop.

Birdie: True. But let me think about it.

Chase: Okay.

Chase: Have a good night, Birdie.

Birdie: You too.

I put my phone on the nightstand, convinced that Janice was right after all. I'm definitely, undoubtedly, playing with fire.

15

———

The next morning, Rhett is already in the kitchen making breakfast when I wake up.

"Hey, baby," he says, turning from the stove. "I'm making you an omelet."

"You are?" Uh-oh. He only makes me breakfast when he wants something.

"Yup. With the works." He comes sweeping over and places a plate in front of me. The omelet is loaded with cheese and veggies, and was clearly made with care. There's even a garnish on the plate, and the sight of it has the red flags in my stomach waving.

"Thanks ..."

I take a bite, then wait for the shoe to drop.

"So, I have good news," he says smiling. "You know those calls I got when we were visiting Chase's shop?"

"Yeah, what about them?"

"It was Dad's firm. They were calling to tell me about an open position under Franklin Starkman. He's an investing genius and has the most impressive portfolio at the company, according to my father. If I got the job, I'd be learning from the best. Working with Franklin would imme-diately put me on the fast track."

"That's amazing," I tell him happily, taking a bite of the omelet. "Sounds like something you can't pass up."

"Exactly. But, see, the thing is ..."

And here it is. The reason he's making me breakfast. I gird my loins. The last time he made me an omelet was when he accidentally threw out a few rolls of my film that I needed for my midterm.

"Franklin works out of the California office."

I cock my head to the side. "How would that work, then? You live here."

"I'd have to move there."

"Oh ..." Move to California? But that would mean ... "Oh."

"And I'd want you to come with me."

I blink at him, feeling like my mind is short-circuiting. Is he serious? "Rhett ... what? I can't move to California."

"Of course you can! Just think of all the fun we'd have! The weather, the beaches, the Hollywood lifestyle. It'd be different, sure, and I know I'm dropping this on you out of nowhere, but ... it feels right, doesn't it?"

"Feels right to whom?" I drop my fork onto my plate and the clatter makes Rhett jump. "Rhett, I love the changing seasons in the Northeast. And we have beaches here, and since when have I ever cared about anything to do with Hollywood? My mom's here and I'm all she has. I'm sorry, but ... I don't want to move to California."

"But this is the opportunity of a lifetime!" He reaches out and grabs my hands. "If you don't like it, we can always come back. I promise. All I'm asking is that you try. For me."

"But what about Chase and the shop?"

He waves me off. "Chase will be self-sufficient by the

time I leave, and I can handle all the business from there. That's not going to be an issue."

"But what about my business with Dasha? We already have our mission statement and mock-ups and have been looking for a place to use as our studio and storefront. I can't just leave her high and dry. I'm sorry, but no. I'm not moving."

His face reddens, and I can tell he's starting to get upset.

"Bird, you can take pictures from anywhere. What does that matter? And let's be honest, were you really going to start a business around *photography*? You guys are a dime a dozen. All you need is an Instagram account to be a photographer."

The minute the words leave his mouth, I can tell he knows he messed up. "Shit, Birdie, I'm sorry. I didn't mean it like that."

I stiffen in my seat. "Yes, you did. You've always looked down on my career choice. Just be honest. You never thought that what I do was as important as what you do."

He scrubs a hand over his face. "Fine, yes. I feel that way … a little. I mean, you know I think the world of your photographs, but I just want more for you. You're so smart and creative, and to waste it on something that literally anyone can do is not what I want for you—"

I hold up a hand. "Stop right there. You're digging yourself into a grave. I'm not listening to another word."

"Birdie, come on. You asked me to be honest, so I was. Please don't overreact."

"I never overreact. In fact, I don't react enough."

"Huh? What are you talking about?"

I'm so mad, I don't even have the energy to explain myself. "I don't want to talk about this anymore. In fact, I need a break. I'm going to Vermont this coming Sunday and I won't be back until Wednesday afternoon."

"A break? Like a real break? From us?" His face falls, but I don't stick around to answer the question. Because the truth is, I don't know. I'm just seeing red and before I make any rash decisions, I need to walk away and think. I slowly back my chair up from the table and leave the room. I'm angry, but I'm hurt too. I always knew what he thought of my career, but to have him confirm it feels like a dagger to the heart.

Photography means so much to me. It's a creative outlet that connects me to my dad, since I can't paint worth a damn. He gave me my first camera and every time I take a decent picture, I think of him. Not only that, but it's my way of living in the moment. When I take photographs of the little things, I can stop myself from letting the loss of my father swallow me whole. Photography is everything to me. It saved my life.

I think about calling Dasha and venting, but I just don't have the energy. What I do instead is pick up my phone and open the text thread with Chase from last night.

Birdie: Leaving Sunday morning if you're still interested.

Chase: What time do we leave?

16

———

The next few days pass by in a blur.

Rhett and I still haven't spoken, and at this point, we're nothing more than two ships passing in the night. We've both been tiptoeing around the apartment, pretending things aren't awkward as hell and avoiding eye contact. He's been spending his nights on the couch, and I haven't given him any openings that I want to try to talk things out.

I've been ignoring Janice's calls too, unable to drum up the energy to deal with her either.

I don't know what to say to either of them, which is the strange part because inside, there is so much I want to get off my chest. There's a voice inside me that's trapped and screaming, but I have no idea how to let her out.

But I can tell that something inside me is definitely thawing, and until I figure out what it is, I'm taking my space from both of them.

My focus right now needs to be this contest and finding the perfect photo. I want to make my father proud, and

winning this contest will start my life and photography business on a high note.

On Sunday morning, I arrive at Chase's apartment bright and early.

We haven't spoken much this past week, other than to figure out logistics. I insisted on driving because it gives me some semblance of control, which I don't have a lot of right now. Since I'll be alone with Chase, I need all the control I can get.

The car door suddenly opens and Chase hops in. He tosses his bag into the backseat, then turns to me with a smile.

I try to smile back, but I probably just look constipated. Already, the car feels too small with him in it.

Ugh. What did I get myself into?

"Good morning," he says, handing me a red Thermos. "This is for you."

"Good morning." I take a sniff and the smell of cinnamon fills my nose. "What's this?"

"My gingerbread latte. It's a new recipe I'm working on. I'd love to hear what you think. And please, be honest."

I take a sip and ... *oh my God*. I take another, then another, and then turn to him with wide eyes. "Chase, this is liquid gold."

He grins, those intense eyes lighting up just a bit. "Good. I brought along a few containers of it for the ride."

"One less stop to make, then." I take another sip and moan. "Screw coffee. This is all I'm drinking for, like, the rest of my life."

He laughs loudly and the deep sound fills the car. Shocked, my head immediately snaps to him. "Did you just laugh? I don't think I've ever heard you laugh."

"I'm just in a good mood, that's all."

A smile tilts my lips. "We'll see if you say that in another few hours. We've got a long drive ahead of us."

He leans back in the seat, keeping his head turned in my direction. "Then we'd better get going."

I put the car into drive and pull out of Chase's street, very much aware of the handsome semi-stranger beside me. The tension that's always between us is there, and I start to wonder if I made a very big mistake by inviting him along. I'm one hundred percent committed to trying to be friends with him, but is this the right way to go about it? Spending five hours—ten if you count the way back—in a car alone with him? Not to mention all the extra time we'll share while I take photos of the area.

And I can't help but wonder what Rhett would do if he found out about this trip. Thinking of Rhett reminds me of California, and a rush of anger has me gripping the steering wheel—

JINGLE BELL, JINGLE BELL, JINGLE BELL ROCK!

The loud music suddenly pumps out of my speakers and scares me so much I nearly swerve off the road.

"Oh, my God!" I reach for the volume knob and turn it down. That's when I realize that Chase is connected to my Bluetooth. I turn to him and his smile is as wide as the Grinch's. "Did you do that on purpose?" I ask him.

"Yes, I did."

"Why?!"

He raises a brow. "One, because I like that song. And two, because you were looking really anxious over there. Road trips are supposed to be fun, so I figured I'd try to lighten the mood. I thought we could use a little Christmas magic."

I shake my head. "You scared the hell out of me. If you want to make it to Vermont alive, warn a girl next time."

He chuckles. "What were you thinking about, anyway?"

I'm not going to tell him that, so I quickly change gears in the conversation. "Chase's Christmas Playlist." I gesture to his phone on the dashboard. "You're a big fan of Christmas music, huh?"

"I listen to it all year round, in fact."

"You do not."

"I do. I even work out to it."

I flick my eyes to him "That is very hard for me to believe. You do not seem like the Christmas-music type."

"Why not?" he asks, sounding offended.

"Because Christmas music is so … jolly. And you're … so …"

"I'm what?"

I laugh. "I don't know. Kind of serious, I guess."

"Maybe I only seem that way. Look, we agreed that we both don't know each other very well. We should fix that if we're actually going to be friends."

I grin at that. "So what, you want to know my favorite movie or something?"

"Sure, but I'd rather you tell me something that will surprise me." He turns to face me fully in the seat. "Try to top my year-round love for Christmas music."

"Hmm … okay." Something immediately comes to mind, but I debate for a second about whether I should tell him. Agh, screw it. "I have a tattoo."

His eyebrows fly up his forehead. "No shit. Where?"

"On my hip. I got it when I was sixteen."

"Wow, aren't you the little rebel? I never would have guessed that."

"It was all Janice's idea. We went to some shady place in New York City that didn't ask questions or require a parent's approval."

Chase's laugh fills the car. "That is shocking. I have to see to this tattoo. What's it of?"

That's the part I don't want to tell him, so I just shrug. "Eh, just something a sixteen-year-old would get."

"Hmm, I think that tops my Christmas-music revelation."

I lean back in my seat and shoot him a smile. "I'm sure you're not going to let me win that easily. Can you top my rebel tattoo?"

"Psh, of course I can." He taps his fingers on his jeans. "So, when I'm alone ..."

His voice is low and deep, seductive almost. I hold my breath, wondering what he's going to say.

"When I'm alone ..." he continues in the same tone. "I like to climb the stairs in a bear crawl."

"YOU WHAT?! What does that even mean?" I'm practically shrieking.

He runs both hands through his hair, and I can tell he's a little embarrassed. "I don't know, it's just fun. I used to do it as a kid and never really grew out of the habit."

"That is SO weird."

"What?! Like you didn't do weird things as a kid?"

My cheeks pink. "I did, come to think of it. I actually think I can top your bear-climbing fetish."

"I'm all ears."

I've never told anyone this secret, and I can't believe I'm about to reveal it now. But oddly, I think it will feel good to get off my chest. "Okay, so when I was little, I carried around a tiny little Barbie suitcase in my pocket." I take a deep breath, already embarrassed. "And in it, I would collect little balls of fuzz from people's carpets. Everywhere I went I would collect a piece of fuzz. I don't know why!"

He barks out a laugh, covering his mouth. "Holy shit. That's fuckin' weird."

"I know!" I shake my head. "I would go home and just look at them and … ugh. Like I said, no idea why I did that."

"Damn," he laughs. "I think you got me on that one."

"So you're saying you can't top that?"

"That sounds like a challenge." He makes a noise like he's thinking, then suddenly straightens. "Oh, this will top them all. When our shop closed down, no one wanted to buy the building, so it fell into disrepair. I'd go back sometimes to be alone, and one night I saw that a few raccoons had made their home there. They looked hungry so I gave them some food."

"Aww," I say. "That's sweet."

"Yeah, well, as you can imagine, they kept coming back. And then word must have spread around the forest, because squirrels started coming, and even a few deer. Pretty soon the place would fill with animals every night after six p.m. Anyway, I'd bring them all food, and when it was really hot in the summer, I set up a kiddie pool, and a little obstacle course from hay bales. We'd all hang out for hours."

"Chase that's … that's …" Stunned, I blink at the road. "Seriously amazing."

He laughs. "It was. Well, until I got caught and they locked the place up."

I turn to him look at him with new eyes. "You were like a modern-day Snow White or something."

"Now the question is … can you top that?"

I can, but I'm not sure it's smart to bring the conversation in this direction. But when I turn and see Chase's smug grin, I decide that it will be worth it.

"I think I can top it. You almost asked my favorite movie. One of them is that old Mark Wahlberg film … *Fear*."

"I've seen it." He quirks a brow. "That's an interesting choice."

"I know, but I liked it because of one scene in particular." My cheeks heat, and I grip the steering wheel. "You know, the one on the rollercoaster?"

The infamous scene where innocent Reese Witherspoon is fingered by the local bad boy. Something about it fascinated me when I was younger, and I couldn't stop watching it.

I can feel Chase's eyes on me. "Interesting," he says. "And what about that scene did you like?"

"I first saw it at twelve and I didn't really understand what was happening. All I knew was that Reese looked really, really happy. Once I found out why, I was even more intrigued. And determined that the same thing should happen to me."

I can hear the smile in is voice. "And did it?"

"Not exactly."

"What do you mean?"

I bite my lip, unable to believe I'm telling him this. "You know Playland Park? That small theme park in New York?"

"Yes …"

"When I was fifteen, I went there with a boy I was kind of dating. I pointed to the Dragon Coaster, and when I told him what I wanted to do, he wasn't into it. He was probably nervous, now that I look back on it, because we hadn't done anything beyond kissing. But either way, he said no. But I was determined, so …"

Chase makes a strangled noise in his throat. "You asked a stranger to finger you?!"

"No!" I half laugh, half shout. "I ... did it myself."

From the corner of my eye, I see his jaw drop. "You masturbated on the Dragon Coaster at Playland?!"

"*Yes!*" I laugh loudly, feeling as crazy as I did that day.

"Did it work?! Did anyone see you?! I have so many questions."

"It did not work, no. And no one saw me, thank God. I'd be a felon if that were the case." I shake my head. "The whole thing was one big fail. But I tried."

"Birdie, that is ... wow."

I playfully shrug one shoulder. "I win."

"I'll say you do." He takes a sip of his gingerbread latte and shifts in his seat. "That's, like, crazy and hot at the same time. I can't decide which one wins out."

"Don't tell anyone!" I warn him. "About that or the Barbie suitcase or anything."

He crosses his heart. "Your weird secrets are safe with me."

We smile at each other briefly before I turn back to the road. Up ahead, there's a sign advertising a local diner, and I realize how hungry I am.

"Did you eat breakfast?" Chase asks, as if reading my mind.

I shake my head and turn on my signal. "Diner?"

"Definitely."

Named for a nearby seaport town, the diner looks like it's about a hundred years old. But the smells wafting out of the building are delicious, and my stomach growls right as I step out of the car. It's freezing outside, and the wind is blowing, so Chase and I hustle to the door.

We're seated in a pink and blue booth that's patched in

places with duct tape, but somehow it adds to the overall appeal of the place.

As I watch Chase browse the menu, my stomach again ties in knots. In the car, we were next to each other, so it was easier to talk without maintaining eye contact. But now that we're face to face, I'm struck by how handsome he is. It's almost unbelievable how the boy I thought about for nearly a decade has somehow transformed into this man sitting before me.

Chase looks up and catches me staring. "What?"

"Nothing." I say embarrassed. "Just ... strange to be here with you, you know?"

He shrugs. "I don't know. I always knew I'd see you again."

"You did?"

"Just a feeling."

"Oh." His words have my fingers tingling, and I busy myself by looking at the menu.

The waiter comes over then, and once we order, I ask Chase a question I've been wondering all week.

"So what's up in Vermont? Are you visiting family?"

He pauses for a second, a shadow passing over his face. "I have a few things to take care of, but yeah, my family still lives up there. I'm taking my sister out to lunch first thing."

"I didn't know you had a sister. How old is she?"

"Twenty-one. It's just her and my dad now. My mom died a few years ago unexpectedly. They found a tumor in her brain but it was too late to operate."

A heavy lead ball forms in the pit of my stomach. "Oh, Chase, I'm so sorry." Thoughts of my own father swirl painfully in my head. I know all too well how Chase must feel. I reach out and put my hand on his. "Seriously. I'm really sorry."

"Thanks. It was hard. Especially on my dad. He's getting up there in age, and can't work like he used to. He has the odd job here and there, but for a few years now, I've been footing most of the bills by doing some catering work. We still owe a lot to the hospital, so I'm hoping the business does well so we can start to make a real dent." He swallows, then shakes his head. "We're a little in over our heads right now. Bill collectors have been calling, and we're running out of time to pay."

My heart squeezes with sympathy. "Chase, I had no idea."

He smiles at me. "Sorry, I don't mean to bring down the mood."

"Don't be sorry." His hand is still in mine, so I squeeze it, just once. Is there anything I can do to help? If there is, please tell me."

His eyes lock onto mine. "You already are helping just by spending time with me and agreeing to be my friend. It makes a tough trip like this that much easier."

I don't look away, even though my heart is pounding. "A tough trip?"

"I have to meet with the financial board at the hospital. See if we can get an extension on some of the loans."

"I see. I'm sorry, Chase." I want to offer him money, but it doesn't feel like the right thing at the moment, so I try to give him what support I can. "You're an incredible son and brother for taking all this on. From what I've seen, your business is a guaranteed success. I have no doubt things will work out for you."

His jaw flexes. "Again, thanks to Rhett."

"No, thanks to you. *You did this.* Rhett is good at what he does, but don't ever think that you haven't earned every bit of your success."

He nods, but then looks down at the table. It's obviously a sensitive topic, so I'm relieved when our food arrives. Hearing about Chase's situation just drives home the fact that I can't mess up anything between him and Rhett. Chase has the weight of the world on his shoulders, a family to take care of, and a host of real-world problems. I'd hate myself if I was the reason everything came crashing down on him.

"Anyway, tell me about your photography," Chase asks, taking a big bite of waffle.

"I'll do you one better," I say. "I'll show you."

I reach into my purse, suddenly nervous. Bringing this picture was a last-minute decision, but I'm suddenly glad I did, especially after our previous conversation. I think Chase will enjoy it, and I know I'm right when I slide it across the table to him. He reaches for it, and as he realizes what it is, his face lights up.

"This is the picture you took of me that night," he says, his voice low.

I nod. "The one I told you I deleted. As you can see, you weren't very happy to see me at first."

He laughs quietly, as his eyes remain locked on the photo. "If I only knew then ..." he muses.

I clear my throat. "It's one of my favorite photos. You can keep it if you want. I made another copy."

He stares down at it, then back up at me. "Thank you. This is the best gift I've ever gotten. I only wish you were in it too."

I blush, happy I was able to lift his mood, even if just a little.

"I can't wait to see more of your photography," Chase starts, tucking the picture into his jacket. "It's fascinating how some people just have an instinct when it comes to taking the right shot. There so much that goes into it, especially during the editing phase, I'm sure. It's really impressive that you have this kind of skill."

"Thank you." His compliment is refreshing, and I can't help but think of Rhett and how he's never once said anything like that about my work. "Speaking of the perfect shot ..."

I spend the next few minutes telling Chase about the holiday contest and how I'm going to Vermont for inspiration.

"This contest must mean a lot to you," he comments afterward, finishing off his food. "Traveling all the way to Vermont seems like a long way to go to find Christmas."

"That's just it ... Vermont is Christmas to me. My dad loved it there. It may seem silly, but he told me there's magic in the woods. Those were basically his last words to me."

"I remember," Chase says meaningfully, his eyes twinkling. "And I'm with your dad. I think there is magic in the woods."

I bite my lip on a smile. "Me too. My dad said he never failed to find inspiration for his work there, so I'm hoping they have the same effect on me."

"His work?"

"My dad was Roy Tenneson."

His eyes go wide. "Get out! That's so cool."

I smile. "So yeah, this contest does mean a lot to me. I want to win to ... make him proud, you know? I'll never be as good as him, but I'd like to try."

Chase grabs my hand this time. "Even if you don't win, I still think he'd be proud."

"And your mom would be proud of you. How could she not be?"

"Thanks. I hope so."

Despite the melancholy conversation over breakfast, the vibe between Chase and me is light when we stand up to leave. When he isn't being all intense or putting me on the spot, he's actually really easy to talk to and be around. I suddenly have high hopes for the rest of the trip.

That is, until I get outside and see an elf standing by my car.

17

It wasn't the kind of elf that's small and cheerful and lives in Santa's workshop.

No, this elf has red and white candy-cane-striped stockings, black high-heeled boots, and a green dress that's so tight her jingle bells are nearly bursting out of it. Chase and I give each other a look before heading to my car. As we get closer, I realize she was the hostess who seated us inside.

"Umm ..." I ask carefully "Can I help you?"

The woman turns and takes us in before speaking. "My ride bailed on me. And I was supposed to be at my other job ten minutes ago. I can't get a rideshare out here worth a damn."

"Oh, I'm sorry," I say.

I do not want to help this woman out—mainly because the way she's suddenly eyeing Chase is borderline obscene. I peer at him, wondering if he finds her attractive. She's in her mid-twenties and has a really great body. It's way more appealing, I'm sure, than my subtle curves. Ugh, why am I even thinking about this? It's not like my nonexistent curves and I are available.

"Where is your job?" I ask, sighing.

But she doesn't respond. She's still ogling Chase, who is now leaning up against my car, his eyes on me.

"You know," she says to him. "The club is looking for a new Santa on Saturday nights. Interested, hot stuff?"

"Club?" Chase asks.

"Yeah. The strip joint right off 95. Pays well."

Chase lets out a shocked laugh. "What? Yeah, no. I don't think so. I'm not a stripper."

"You won't have to do much. I know a lot of people who would pay just to sit on that lap of yours."

My jaw and my keys drop at the same time. "Okay," I say, flustered. "We'll give you a ride to work. Is it far from here?"

"Nope," she says, already opening my backseat. "Ten minutes or so."

Ten minutes too long, if you ask me. When I open my driver's side door, all I can smell is her cloying perfume. Why the hell did I offer her a ride? I have places to be. I start the car a little rougher than usual, and when Chase's light chuckle reaches my ears, I shoot him a frustrated stare. What is he laughing about anyway?

The woman leans up in between our seats, forcing me to hold my breath so I'm not assaulted by her smell. She gives me directions, but then unfortunately does not lean back.

"So, how long you guys been together?" she asks conversationally.

"We're not together. We're just friends," I respond, annoyed.

Her answering squawk makes me jump. "Friends? With this guy? What, do you like the clam or something?"

"What? No!" I respond, outraged. "I ... I have a boyfriend."

"Is he better looking than this guy?"

Chase turns to me and raises a brow as if he, too, is interested in the answer. I shake my head. "I'm not answering that."

"I'll take that as a no. Anyway, I'm single," she purrs, leaning closer to Chase, "in case you were interested."

Chase still looks amused about something. "I'm not really the relationship type."

"I didn't say I was interested in a relationship ..."

"We're here!" I say, my face red. Honestly, how inappropriate can this woman be? She literally just propositioned Chase in my car after knowing him for two seconds.

The woman laughs. "Bummer. If you are ever interested, big guy, you know where to find me. The name's Candy Cane."

"Of course it is," I grumble under my breath.

I watch her shimmy out of the car in my rearview mirror. She leans back in once more and smiles at us. "Thanks. I owe you both one. I would hate to have walked, especially with the snow coming."

"Snow? What snow?" I ask.

She gives me a look. "It's December in New England. Don't you look up the weather?"

With one more look at Chase, she slams the door and walks away.

"Shit," Chase says, eyes on his phone. "We've got a big storm behind us."

"How many inches?"

"Enough." He grimaces. "This sucks. We've barely even gotten started."

"Let's get as far as we can," I say, pulling out of the parking lot. "Try to outrun it."

And for a few hours, we're able to stay just one step ahead of the storm. But by early afternoon, big fat flakes start falling onto the windshield. I can tell by the look of it that it isn't going to be a light snow that will just leave a pretty, thin coating on the trees. It's the type of snow that piles up quick and makes driving dangerous.

"Shit," I say, slowing down a bit. "We're still a few hours from Vermont."

Chase looks up something on his phone, then sighs. "Yeah, we're not going to make it."

"Ugh. So what do we do?"

"We're going to have to find a hotel."

"If there's one even around here," I say, reading the nearest sign. We're somewhere in the middle of nowhere, Massachusetts.

I suddenly hiss when my tires slip a bit on the ice. I know we have to find something—and fast.

Chase leans over to show me his screen. "There's a small B&B about three miles from here on the shoreline. It looks all right, and isn't too expensive."

"Works for me. Just tell me how to get there."

The three-mile drive takes us double the time it normally would.

"Man, it's really coming down," Chase says as I finally pull into the B&B. "Shame on us for not seeing this coming."

He's right about that. But I know why I didn't bother checking the weather. I was too distracted with the fact that Chase was coming on this trip and my problems with Rhett to worry about something like whether or not there'd be snow. God, I'm an idiot. "At least we made it here safely."

And at least the B&B is adorable. Nestled against the sea, the Womack Shore B&B is a lot better than I thought it would be. It's a two-story house made of both stone and bright red brick, and it has a wide wraparound porch and a large blue door. Blue and white twinkle lights outline the picket fence out front, and I imagine at night it's a sight to see. There's a candle in every window, and a wreath on every door. It's cozy, and way better than any motel would be.

"Good find," I say, turning off the car. "It sucks we're going to miss a day in Vermont, though."

"Nothing we can do about that." Chase gets out of the car and heads for the trunk. "Here, let me grab your bags."

I smile at him. "Thanks."

Walking up to the B&B with Chase is strange. Anyone watching us from the outside would definitely think we're a couple. Candy Cane certainly did. I hurry up the steps and put a little distance between us, unsure how I feel about that.

When I open the door and step inside, I'm greeted by a blast of warmth, and I don't mean just the temperature. The Christmas décor inside is ocean-themed, and even though it's not what I'm used to, there's something really festive about it. More blue and white twinkle lights line the furniture and wainscoting. Miniature Christmas trees made of sea glass dot the front desk, and wreaths crafted out of starfish and seashells hang on the back of the doors. There's a large bowl of ornaments filled with sand on a side table, and stockings decorated with anchors and seahorses wearing Santa hats hang from the mantle. A low of hum of holiday music is playing in the background, and there's a smell of peppermint on the air.

My eyes are drawn to the old woman behind the front desk. She's in a ruffled red and green apron with a sprig of holly in her hair. She reminds a little of Mrs. Claus, and I can't help but smile.

"Welcome!" she calls out, waving us in. "Come on in out of that cold. And make sure to close that door behind you. We're in for a doozy out there."

"Is it supposed to last all night?" I ask, approaching the desk. I eye the keys hanging on the wall behind her, and when I see only one, the tension in my gut builds.

"Not all night. It's supposed to stop around eleven. They say it'll be short and not so sweet, though. We're in for at least a foot."

"Hope you have a shovel," Chase says, putting our bags down by our feet. "And a couple of rooms for the night. I saw on the website you had vacancies."

The woman smiles. "I have a shovel that you may borrow if you'd like. But as for the rooms, we've only got one left."

I knew it. Of course this has to play out like some romantic comedy where the two main characters are stuck sharing a room, and then are forced to live through a series of awkward moments and comedic errors. Ugh. I refuse to make this weird. Chase and I are friends. We can share a room, for God's sake.

I can feel Chase looking at me, and when I turn to meet his eyes, I see the question there. I give him a soft smile and turn back to the woman.

"We'll take it."

18

After a small battle with the skeleton key, Chase and I shuffle into the room with our bags. It's small. Really small, and the bed, while comfortable-looking, can't be bigger than a full.

"I'll sleep on the floor," Chase says instantly, his mind obviously in the same place mine is.

"It's freezing. You can't sleep on the floor."

But I'm starting to think that maybe he should. When we close the door behind us and are enveloped in silence, the ever-present tension between us grows.

I walk around to the other side of the bed, needing to put a little space between us.

Chase suddenly smiles, gesturing to the ceramic Christmas tree on his nightstand. "My grandma had one of these."

I giggle. "I think every grandmother had one. Mine passed hers down to my mom, and we still put it up every year."

He sits down on the bed, still watching me. "So are you a

fan of Christmas now? You weren't when I met you, but I know that back then, things were ... hard."

I'm a big fan of Christmas now, because of him. He taught me to live in each snowflake-filled moment and focus on the joy the season brings. But I'm way too shy to tell him that now. Especially when we're holed up in this room together without any space to think. "Things are still hard sometimes, but, yeah. I do like Christmas. It's my favorite holiday."

"Good." He moves to pick up a pamphlet left on his pillow. "If you're feeling festive, what do you say we grab something to eat tonight at this Christmas-themed bar? It's next door so we can walk."

"Sounds good to me. But if our waitress is named Candy Cane, I'm going to lose it."

Chase laughs loudly, then leans back on his pillow. "Do you mind if I try to take a small nap before then? I didn't get much sleep last night."

"How come? Last-minute packing?"

"Nope," he says, not meeting my eyes. "Just excited about the trip, I guess."

My stomach flips. "Oh. I don't mind at all. In fact, a nap isn't a bad idea. We were up early this morning."

I take off my winter coat and gloves, and Chase does the same. My cheeks are bright red, and I can't blame it on the weather. If the other stuff felt domestic, stripping simultaneously across a bed from Chase feels downright sinful. As soon as I can, I pull down the covers and slide into bed, making sure to stay as close to the edge as possible.

A few seconds later, the bed sinks with weight as Chase climbs in. He flicks off the light, and a warm glow suffuses the room.

To say I'm on edge would be an understatement. No way

I'm falling asleep like this. My body feels like it's connected to a live wire. Electrified, my dad used to say.

So when Chase suddenly starts laughing, I nearly jump out of my skin.

"What?" I ask. "What is it?"

"Look."

I shift over onto my back and lean up on my hands. Chase is pointing to the wall in front of us, and when I see what he's pointing at, I laugh too.

"No way. Is that a moose?"

"I think so."

I take in the medium-sized wooden statue standing on the dresser, feeling a sense of déjà vu.

"Our second moose sighting," Chase says, turning to me. "I think it's a sign."

I raise a brow. "A sign of what?"

He just shrugs, a mischievous grin on his face.

"It's not a sign," I say. "Just a coincidence."

At least, that's what I'm telling myself. I lie back down, still feeling an electric current running through my system. But eventually, I'm lulled to sleep by the sound of Chase's light snoring.

I wake to the sounds of movement, and when I raise my head, Chase is just coming out of the bathroom, dressed in a sweater and jeans. "Sorry, didn't mean to wake you," he says.

My stomach growls, and I laugh. "My appetite would have done it soon anyway. You ready for dinner?"

Chase nods, his eyes intense as he looks me over. Even though I'm dressed, I feel stripped bare, feeling like we're in the middle of another impromptu domestic moment.

I smile at him and get out of bed, then head over to my suitcase. Once I pull out new clothes, Chase gives me a small wave. "I'll wait for you by the main entrance."

"Sounds good."

He leaves a second later and I heave a sigh of relief. I can't believe I just slept in the same bed as Chase. The good thing is, I was able to do so without drowning in sexual tension. Maybe this whole friends thing is going work out after all.

Feeling confident, I get dressed, then head to the main entrance. Chase is there, talking to the old woman, who definitely has hearts in her eyes as she stares at him. I don't blame her. He looks hot in his red and green sweater and black leather jacket. He looks warm and cheerful all at once, like a really, really sexy elf.

He spots me over her shoulder and smiles. "Ready?"

"Definitely."

"Have fun, you two," the woman calls out, waving us to the door. "And be careful on the ice. It's slippery!"

"We will," I say, waving goodbye.

When we open the door, we're hit by a blast of cold air. The snow is really coming down now, and of course I didn't pack the proper shoes. It's just me and my ankle booties again. What was I thinking?

"Here, lean on me," Chase says and offers his arm.

"No, it's okay. I'll be fine."

I shouldn't be leaning on him. Everything is going so well, and I'm afraid if I even so much as touch him, it will rock the boat. But I swear as soon as I turn down his offer, my foot slips on the bottom stair and I have to grab his arm anyway.

Chase chuckles. "Careful. You okay?"

"I'm fine." Embarrassed, but fine. And just as I thought, Chase feels incredible. His arm is just so warm. I can feel the heat of his skin even through my gloves, and it's all I can do not to lean into him further.

Luckily, we make it across the parking lot without any further incident, and when we get to the door, I reluctantly let go of his arm.

The bar is named Rudolph's Road House, and just like the B&B, it's decked out completely in Christmas décor. There are large plastic Mr. and Mrs. Claus statues by the front door, red and green lights crisscrossed over the ceiling beams, and retro Santa memorabilia hanging on the walls. It's kitschy, but it's charming at the same time. And while the whole place looks like it could use a major dusting, there's still a roaring fireplace, a wide oak bar, and smells wafting from the kitchen that have my stomach growling.

We're seated by a man named Thomas and given menus loaded with pub fare.

"This is my type of place," Chase says.

I look up from my menu and meet his eyes. He's across from me, but the table is small, so it sort of feels like we're on top of one another. It makes the whole thing feel like a date, so I quickly avert my eyes and look back down at my menu.

Chase sighs. "I wish you would relax."

"What do you mean?"

"You're uncomfortable. I get it. You have a boyfriend, and here you are, sharing a room and a meal with another man. But you don't have to worry. I would never try anything with you that you didn't want. I'm a good guy. Can you just try to remember that, so you don't have to sit there like you have the world's biggest wedgie?"

I think about denying it, but what's the point? "Sorry. I guess this all feels a little weird."

"I know. But we're here, and we have to make the best of the situation. So let's try to have fun. As friends. What do you say?"

I nod and meet his eyes, sensing that he's being genuine. "Okay. I can do that."

"A glass of wine might help."

I snort. "Or two."

The waiter comes over then and after we put it our orders and our drinks are set down, I finally do start to relax.

"So, tell me more about yourself," Chase says, taking a sip of his bourbon.

"I think I told you plenty of wild things in the car, don't you?"

He laughs. "True enough. But tell me the more boring stuff now. Like your favorite show and how you like to spend your free time. You know, the things that friends know about each other."

"Okay. Well, my favorite show is *Game of Thrones* ..."

For the next twenty minutes, Chase and I get to know each other as friends. We both love fantasy series and hate romantic comedies. We both would prefer a night in instead of going out, and we both love to travel. We have a lot in common, despite our obvious differences.

It's funny, because getting to know him this way kind of feels like going backwards. Chase and I had such a connection the night we met. It cemented itself inside both of us and it's still there today, so it's kind of weird to talk about trivial things like TV shows with him. It turns out that we have a ton of mutual interests, but even if we didn't, I'd still want to be his friend. That kind of connection we had way back then matters, and I'm not about to let it go.

Our food is brought over along with another round of drinks, and the tension between us seems to fade into the background as we just enjoy ourselves.

But when our dishes are cleared away and Chase leans over, I sense the energy around us shifting. "I want to ask you a question, and you have to answer it honestly," he tells me.

"Okay, I'll do my best."

"Were you jealous today? Of Candy Cane?"

I scoff into my glass. "Jealous of a stripper? No way."

One side of his mouth turns up. "I don't know. You seemed a little ... on edge when she was flirting with me."

"Because it was borderline sexual harassment. I'm surprised you weren't uncomfortable."

"I wasn't paying attention. I was too busy watching you."

His words give me a rush, but then the alarm bells in my head starts ringing. "Chase, don't start."

"Okay, sorry." He holds both hands up. "Just being honest. I swear. I really am trying to hold myself back for your sake and give this whole friends thing a shot. I wouldn't want to come between you and Rhett. Not this way."

I take another sip of wine. "You're not what's coming between me and Rhett."

His eyes narrow. "What do you mean by that?"

I know I shouldn't say anything, especially to Chase, but it's been sitting in the back of my mind for the past week, and I need to get it out. "Rhett wants us to move to California once we graduate. He has a great job offer there, but I don't want to go. I don't know, maybe I'm being selfish. I just, among other things, don't want to be around palm trees at Christmastime."

"Sorry to hear that," Chase says after a beat. "Sounds like you're in a tough spot."

I raise a brow. "Are you actually sorry?"

"Honestly, yes and no." He takes another sip of his drink and smiles at me. "I definitely don't want to see you hurt. But ... well, you know."

Ours eyes lock, and that tension starts building up between us again. I look away, trying to stay on track.

"I'm not sure what I'm going to do yet, but I'll figure it out. I just need some space, so this Vermont trip couldn't have come at a better time. He and I are actually on a break right now."

Chase's eyebrows fly up his forehead. "Seriously? Like, you're broken up?"

"I wouldn't say that, exactly."

"What would you say?" he pushes.

"I don't know." Frustration starts to well within me. "I haven't figured it out yet."

His eyes conspicuously drop to my lips. "I didn't know you were single, Birdie."

"I don't know that I am."

Suddenly Chase's eyes change. I see hope, mixed with determination.

"Break up with him. Make it a real break."

I stare at him in shock, my irritation building. "I can't just do that."

"Why not? Birdie, you have no idea how I feel about you. There's something between us, and I think we should—"

I shake my head and close my eyes. "Stop right there. You said you wouldn't do this."

"But—"

"What about giving this friends thing a real shot? I thought you were on board with that."

"Yeah, that was before I knew you were single. This changes things."

I rub the sides of my forehead. "For the last time, I'm not single. I don't know what I am. Rhett is still important to me, and I'm not going to do anything to hurt him."

I shout the words louder than I mean to, and a few other

customers turn in our direction. It's incredibly embarrassing and my irritation rises.

"I'm tired," I say next, without looking at him. "I'm going to head back."

"Damn." Chase leans forward and reaches for my hand, but I pull it away. "Birdie, I'm sorry."

"Just forget it."

I think about storming out of the restaurant completely, but I don't want to make more of a scene than I already have. So I wait in silence while we get the bill, which I insist on splitting evenly, and then walk with him out into the icy air. I hardly feel the cold this time, though. It's nothing compared to how frigid the tension has become between us.

It's not even him I'm mad at. It's myself. Because while I really do want to be his friend, I can't be sure that I'm not subconsciously sending him mixed signals. In fact, I know I am. And it's not fair to anyone. Not to me, not to Chase, and not to Rhett.

I'm also mad at myself because I'm tempted to do exactly what he said and break up with Rhett. Then I could use this time with Chase to explore what's between us. But I know that would be wrong and would only lead to more regrets. I'm not a shady person and I don't want to start by sneaking around behind Rhett's back—break or no break.

I can't help but think that this trip was a mistake. Once Chase and I are sequestered back in our small, very cramped room, that point is driven home even further.

I grab my clothes and head for the bathroom, unable to take the tension between us that seems like a constant haunt over my shoulder.

When I reenter the room, Chase is already in bed with the light off, and he's lying as far from the middle as possible. It can't be comfortable for him, so despite the fact that his eyes are closed, I know he's not sleeping.

A part of me wants to apologize for sending those mixed signals. It's plain as day that Chase wants me, and here I am, inviting him on trips to Vermont and sleeping in the same bed with him and tempting fate.

There's nothing I can do about it now, though, so I have no choice but to simmer in the consequences of my actions.

I turn off my bedside lamp and crawl into bed. Chase's body heat has made the covers warm, and I secretly take advantage of that and snuggle in further.

It takes me a while to fall asleep, and I can tell Chase is awake too. Maybe I should say something. Maybe I should clear the air between us.

But I don't. Because I don't know what to say and the words just won't come.

19

———

The next morning when I wake up, Chase is already gone and out of bed. I roll over and place my hand on the place where he slept and it's cold. He must have gotten a really early start.

It's then that I notice the note on my bedside table.

"Gingerbread latte ready to go in the coffee maker. —Chase."

Leave it to him to do something sweet when I don't deserve it.

After grabbing a cup, I head for the window, and a quick peek outside finds Chase shoveling out my car. There's a lot of snow on the ground, but the sun is shining, so luckily, we should be able to get to Vermont with no problems.

Twenty minutes later, I approach him with a tentative smile and hand him a muffin I got from the kitchen. Our eyes meet briefly, and in his, I see caution and regret.

"It's not as good as your Merry Muffins, but it's not half bad," I tell him softly.

He watches me as he takes a bite. "Thanks. Are you ready to go?"

"Yup. Bags are on the porch."

"I'll go grab them."

He walks by and I almost hold out a hand to stop him, but I let him go. I still don't have the words to say to him. They're still all frozen inside me, so for right now, it's best that I don't say anything at all.

Chase returns with the bags a few minutes later, and after warming up the car, we're off.

He asked to drive, and now that we're underway, I regret saying yes. At least driving would have been a distraction and would have given me something to do. I sneak a glance at him and see that his eyes are totally focused on the road. I can't help but wonder if he had the same idea.

For the next few hours, we don't talk much aside from necessities, and while there's definitely tension between us, it seems to be lying dormant. I'd like to think it's gone, but I know somewhere deep in my gut that it's not.

There's such a dark cloud over the trip now, that once I see the sign welcoming us to Vermont, the excitement I feel takes me by surprise. So much so, I forget that Chase and I aren't speaking.

"Vermont! We made it!" I cheer.

Chase laughs, his eyes sparkling when he looks at me.

"You must be happy to be home," I say.

He nods. "I am. I really miss it here sometimes."

"Why did you open a shop in Connecticut instead of up here?"

"It was Rhett's call, but he was right. I need to start in a densely populated area if I want to make waves. Maybe if things work out in New Haven, and I can get to the point where I can expand, I'll think about putting roots back down here."

"Things are going to work out. I know it."

He turns to me and smiles. It's his curved real smile, and I wonder if we're going to make up now. My eyes are drawn to the curl in the middle of his forehead. I have the strangest desire to reach out and touch it, but manage to stop myself just in time.

He opens his mouth to respond, but then my phone buzzes with a text. It's on the console, and the name RHETT on the screen is obvious. Chase sighs deeply, then turns back to road. After a minute, I grab my phone and open the text.

Rhett: I miss you.

I stare at the words, feeling a strange mix of emotions. He probably does miss me, and I almost cave and respond to him, because I miss him a little bit too. But something stops me at the last minute.

I *always* cave. I always bury my true feelings down deep, and this time I don't want to. Not after the compromise he just expected me to make. And not after what he said about my photography.

I leave the text unanswered, and when I put my phone down, something inside me thaws a little bit more.

I think about saying something to Chase, but he seems closed off again. It's so awkward, and we don't say another word for the rest of the drive.

That is, until we get to Mistletoe Cabin.

It's a traditionally built log cabin home, but a far cry from Laura Ingalls Wilder's little house in the big woods. The entire front of the three-story property is made up of floor-to-ceiling glass windows, and I can see inside to the great room from the driveway. The center-piece of it all is a massive stone hearth that rises up through the vaulted ceilings. Just looking at the home brings back memories of my dad sitting before the fire on Christmas Eve, his mind seemingly a million miles away.

And the view is just as I remembered it to be. There's a spectacular backdrop of large white-tipped Vermont mountains. How could I not find a photo up here? I look around, suddenly eager to get started.

Chase makes a noise beside me, bringing me back to the present.

"This place is something else," he says, staring up at it. "I used to dream about staying here. I'd walk here from my house and imagine what it would be like."

There's a sadness in his eyes, and I suddenly have to desperate urge to fix it. And to fix things between us. "So stay here," I tell him.

He smiles and shakes his head. "I think sticking to the original plan is best. Besides, my dad's house is just a couple of miles away."

"But there are plenty of rooms here. We wouldn't have to share. Come on, I have the whole thing to myself. I could use the company."

He looks back and forth between the house and me. "Okay. I'll stay with my dad and sister tonight, and then stay here Tuesday."

"Perfect. We can come back here after we take the photos for your shop."

"Sounds like a plan." He smiles. "Thanks."

I smile back, and while everything doesn't feel fixed between us, at least it's a start.

I get out of the car and start gathering my bags. We agreed that Chase would drop me off here, then borrow my car, since he's the one who needs to get around and do a few things. As for me, I don't plan on leaving the house for the next day or so, and I wouldn't have it any other way.

"Okay, well, until tomorrow, I guess," I tell him, trying to keep my tone light.

"Until tomorrow," he responds.

And then Chase is driving away, and I'm left standing there with my bags at my feet.

I walk up to the cabin, feeling my dad all around me. After letting myself in, I spend a nostalgic hour exploring the home and taking photos. I can see my dad bounding down the stairs on Christmas morning, as excited as a child. I see my mom on the front porch wrapped in a cardigan, sipping coffee from her holly leaf mug. I see myself sprawled on the shag rug, playing with whatever new toy I'd gotten that year. So many wonderful memories are hidden in this house. It's full of so many moments long past that are etched on my heart.

But I also see myself running out the back door and into the woods, tears streaming down my face with a heart full of grief. The pain of that last Christmas at Mistletoe Cabin is not lost on me either. I think about going back to the tree where I met Chase, but dusk is falling, and I don't want to risk getting lost.

So I spend the night in the front of the fire, eating Chinese takeout and going through the pictures I took that day. There's a nice one of the cabin that I think would look great in Chase's shop, so I flag it to show him. I also send it to my mom with a text saying: *Guess where I am?*

She's going to be so surprised, and maybe a little bit sad. She loved it here too, but she was the one who suggested we stop coming after Dad died. The memories of my father were probably too much to bear.

My phone buzzes with a text, but it's not from my mom. It's Chase.

Chase: You okay over there?

Birdie: I am. I had a nice day. How about you?

Chase: Things worked out. The hospital gave me another few months.

Birdie: That's great news! Did you tell your family? They must be so happy you're home.

Chase: I did. And yeah, they were happy to see me. Probably because I'm going to cook for them.

Birdie: I'm jealous. You guys will be eating better than I am.

I take a picture of my Chinese takeout and send it to him.

Chase: I'll cook for you tomorrow. How does that sound?

Birdie: Sounds great.

He doesn't respond again, so I try to push him out of my mind. I don't need to focus on what's going on between us. Instead, I send a quick text off to Rhett, letting him know I'm okay, but I don't respond to his "I miss you" message.

I head upstairs to the master bedroom, choosing to sleep on the side where my dad slept. I lie on the pillow, wishing he were here and feeling a little bit like he is. That thought makes me smile, and just as I drift off to sleep, I swear I see a sparkle in the window outside.

Hold up. What the heck is that?

I jump out of bed and run to the window. I press my face against the glass, unable to believe what I'm seeing.

There's a sparkle, all right. And for a wonderful second, I wonder if it's the Christmas star. But it's way, way too low to be a star.

No matter how hard I squint, I can't tell what it is. So, making a snap decision, I run to the door, barely remembering to grab my coat.

The back door slams behind me as I jog into the backyard and toward the woods. The moon is bright, but I can

still make out the sparkle. It's right above the tree line, beck-
oning me forward. As I get closer, the sparkle gets brighter
and brighter.

A part of me wonders if I'm imagining this. Could I be
sleepwalking right now? Is this some sort of dream?

My pulse picks up as I jog the remaining distance. But
when I get to the tree line where the sparkle was hovering,
it's gone. There's no light. In fact, it's really, really dark. For
the next few minutes I stand there, wondering what it was
that I saw and getting more disappointed by the second.
Obviously, this is the work of my overactive imagination.
That light was probably just some spotlight a park ranger
set up to keep animals away from the house. Typical me,
seeking out magic where there is none.

Feeling defeated, I start to make my way to the tree line
and back toward the house.

But that's when I see it. A small glint on the ground a few
feet ahead of me. I bend down, and after brushing away the
dirt and grass, my heart leaps into my throat.

It's my Christmas star necklace. The one my dad bought
me, and I lost.

Tears prick my eyes and my bottom lip starts quivering.
My dad and I spent so much time in this woods. I must have
been playing and lost it out here somehow. I unhook the
clasp and put it around my neck, my heart so full I feel as if
it might burst.

I think of my dad's last words to me.

There's magic in the woods.

And for the first time ever, I've seen it for myself.

20

———

The next morning, I wake just as the sun is coming up. Chase won't be here until noon, so I have the perfect opportunity to explore the woods and hopefully take some photos. I'm riding high after finding my necklace last night, and feeling like anything is possible.

My necklace could survive years in the woods without it being disturbed, only for me to happen upon it later, and that's nothing short of a miracle. I clasp the necklace now between two fingers, feeling more hopeful than I have in days.

I head for the forest and find myself following the same path I did as a girl on the Christmas Eve that I met Chase. I'm assaulted not just by visual memories, but sensory memories too. The way the fresh fallen snow smells, the way the branches feel as they snag against my clothing. It all takes me back to how I felt that night. Scared, alone, lost.

It dawns on me that I'm still feeling a little lost. I still freeze when I'm confused, or when I'm unsure of what to say and lacking the courage to say it. But I'm not that scared little girl that I once was. And that's all thanks to Chase and what happened here so long ago.

Ten minutes later, I'm in front of the tree where I met him.

It's just as large and stoic as I remembered it to be.

As I approach, an intense, otherworldly sense of déjà vu rolls through me. The feeling is enhanced because Chase is there, sitting in the same place I found him the first time. As if on reflex, I reach for my camera and snap his photo.

It gets his attention and he looks up. And when our eyes meet, mutual disbelief passes between us.

"What are you doing here?" he asks, stunned.

"I wanted to get a picture of the tree," I say, walking toward him. "What are you doing here?"

He shakes his head. "I'm doing what I always do. I'm here to think."

I nod, trying to hold back a smile. What are the odds we find ourselves here again at the same time?

"Am I interrupting?" I ask.

"Of course not." He grins, patting the space beside him.

I drop to the ground, just like I did that night. The déjà vu feeling is so strong, it almost feels as if I'm playing a part in a movie. The whole thing feels surreal, like an out-of-body experience. When we both turn to each other at the same time, I'm transported back to that moment—the moment that changed my life forever. There's something about this place. Something about *him* that unlocks the words from my throat.

"I'm really sorry about the other night," I whisper.

"No, I'm sorry," he breathes out. "I was totally out of line. It's just ..."

"It's just what?"

"I know I shouldn't pressure you. It's the last thing I want to do. I just feel so … connected to you. I've wanted you for so long, and now that you're back in my life, it's so hard for me to accept that we don't even have a chance to explore our potential together. I don't know. It's hard to explain."

I turn to face him fully. "You don't have to explain. I know what you mean. I've always felt connected to you. You changed my life that day."

He cocks his head to the side. "I did?"

I hold a hand out, imagining a snowflake falling into it. "You taught me how to live in the moment. Whenever I feel overwhelmed, I imagine the snowflake. I focus on the split second between breaths, when you can see its beauty and its magic. That advice not only helped me deal with the loss of my father, but it's helped me get through so many other hard times. You gave me an invaluable gift that night. And I'm so happy that I have the chance to say thank you."

Chase lets out a long, slow breath. "But it's me who should be thanking you. Because you gave me something special that night too."

"I did?" I ask, mimicking his words.

He nods. "When I met you that night, my world was crumbling around me. The shop was closing and we had no money. And yeah, I was sad because I got broken up with, but the truth is I was mostly upset because I knew that I had nothing to give my family on Christmas morning, and I knew they had nothing to give me. But then you came along and gave me something I hadn't had for a long time. Hope." He reaches out and grabs my hand. "Because if something as wonderful as meeting you in that exact moment could happen to me, then I thought that maybe my life wasn't going to be so bad. Maybe there was more out there. I just had to find it. So yeah, I'm the one who should be thanking you."

I blink away tears. "It's crazy how one small moment in time can mean so much."

Just like we did that night, we move toward one another at the same time and pull each other into a hug. I melt into his arms. There's no other word for it.

Having him around me like this, holding him close, it thaws something large and aching inside me.

"I *am* sorry," he whispers against my neck.

Squeezing him tight to me, I shake my head. "So am I. But let's just forget it and move on."

We pull back at the same time, accidentally bringing our mouths inches apart. I stare into his eyes, and the magnetic pull between us is almost impossible to ignore. The air shimmers around us, and the sounds of the forest sound like a melody to my ears.

My heart pounds, unable to keep up with the intensity of the moment. And just when I think I can't take it any longer, Chase's eyes move and fix on something over my shoulder.

"No way," he whispers. "Birdie, look."

I turn around, and when I see the moose, my jaw drops. It can't be. We both stare at it in silence, completely transfixed.

It's not close to us, like it was that first night. It's about twenty feet away, standing on top of a snowy outcrop. Its large majestic antlers appear as a silhouette against a rising sun. A chill runs over my skin, and I can't help but think of my dad.

"Oh, my God," I whisper. "That's it. That's the same one."

I scramble up as carefully as I can, adjust my camera settings with shaking fingers, then snap the picture. I know instinctively that I'm going to submit it for the holiday photo contest, before I even see its negative. This image—this feeling—is Christmas for me. It's perfect. It's my dad, it's magic, it's memories, and it's Chase all rolled into one.

I take a few more shots, just to be safe, and then I turn back to Chase, beaming. "I got it!" I whisper. "The picture I need. That's it!"

He's grinning too. He takes my hand and we rush away from our spot, safely away into the woods, before the moose can see us. When we reach a new cluster of trees and the moose is out of sight, he says, "I think your dad was right. There is magic in these woods. What are the odds we came here at the same time? What are the odds we see another moose? It's like ... fate or something. Real live fate."

"There is magic," I reply, touching my necklace. "It's here."

The tension between us starts closing in again, and my eyes flick to his lips. I can tell he notices, because his jaw flexes and his eyes flash. I want to look away, but it's as if I have no control.

He doesn't make a move, and neither do I. The step feels too big, and the fall would be too great. I'm scared, and I sense he is too.

And then my phone rings, startling us both. After taking a deep breath, I answer. "Hey, Mom."

"Sweetie, are you okay? What are you doing at Mistletoe?"

"I needed some inspiration for the holiday photo contest." I peek over at Chase. He's looking out into the woods, as if scouring the landscape for another moose. "Are you okay, Mom? I was worried when I didn't hear back from you."

"I was busy, and uh, someplace without service. Anyway, how's it going? Did you find the photo?"

"I did." I grin, feeling a bit euphoric. "I think so, anyway."

"Congratulations, sweetie! Tell me everything."

I tell her about the moose and a little about my trip, including the snowstorm. But I don't mention Chase. I'm not ready to open that can of worms. I have no idea what she would think about us coming here together, and I'm in too good of a mood to find out.

When I turn back to Chase after ending the call, I see that he's watching me. He smiles, stuffing both hands in his pockets. "Ready to go?"

"Yeah." I look around once more, still feeling like the air is shimmering. "I'm ready. I just want to take a couple of photos of the tree for your shop."

"Okay, I'll meet you at Mistletoe in a half an hour or so, and then we can head into town. I have some ideas for photos."

"Great. See you then."

He turns to go, but I call out to him. There's one more thing I just have to ask him. "Chase?"

"Yes?"

"Do you think we'll ever come back here? Like, together?"

The question sounds dumb now that I've said it out loud, but I don't regret asking it—especially when he responds with the words I'm hoping to hear. "Yes, I do."

21

When the cabin doorbell rings half an hour later, I nearly jump out of my skin. I forgot how loud the bell can be.

I walk out of the master bedroom and lean over the railing. Chase is on the other side of the door with his bag slung over his shoulder.

"Come on in!" I yell.

After a moment, the knob turns and Chase steps inside. I walk down the winding staircase, enjoying the range of emotions playing across his face.

"Wow," he says, putting his bag down. "This place is incredible."

"Isn't it?" I say. Feeling giddy, I skip the rest of the way down the stairs, then grab his hand and pull him toward the back of the house. "I'll give you a full tour in a few, but I wanted to show you this first."

We pass the den, the bathroom, and a downstairs bedroom, and stop in front of a set of wooden swinging doors.

"Are you ready?" I ask.

He chuckles. "I don't know."

I laugh, pushing against the door with my butt and pulling him inside.

And just as I hoped, the sight of the kitchen has him starry-eyed.

Unlike the rest of the cozy cabin, the kitchen is filled with modern stainless-steel appliances, and an island the size of two dining room tables. There's every gadget you can imagine, along with three fridges and two stoves. It's a chef's paradise, and from the look on Chase's face, it's obvious that's exactly what he's thinking.

"This is ... wow," he sputters, running his hand over the island. "I wasn't expecting this."

"Mistletoe is full of surprises," I tell him, hopping up on a stool. "Don't forget you promised to cook for me tonight."

"It's going to be my pleasure," he says, walking toward the stove. "Seriously."

"We can pick up some ingredients in town," I say, smiling. "Now, how about a full tour?"

He nods, and the lightness in his usually serious face makes me smile. I lead him back out the kitchen, but he stops at the bedroom just outside it. "Can I stay in this room?" he asks.

"You can stay wherever you want," I tell him. "But don't you want to see the other bedrooms first?"

"I'm sure they're nice, but this one will do just fine."

"Okay," I shrug, then lead him back into the main part of the house.

After giving him a full tour, it's safe to say Chase is just as much in love with Mistletoe as I am.

"It's even better than I imagined," he tells me as we're heading to my car half an hour later. "Thanks for letting me stay here."

"Like I said, I'm happy to have the company. We can light a fire later and maybe watch a Christmas movie."

Chase shakes his head just as he gets into the driver's side.

"What is it?" I ask.

"Nothing."

"Tell me," I say, getting into the passenger seat and smiling at him.

"Cooking for you, sitting in front of a fire, watching a Christmas movie together ... it's like you just described my perfect night."

I blush, then bite my lip. "That's sweet, Chase."

"You're sweet," he responds, clearing his throat and looking away. "Especially because you're helping me take these photos for my shop."

"It's the least I can do for the amazing meal I'm sure to get tonight."

He laughs and we chat lightly as we make the fifteen-minute drive into town. The first place he takes me is an old, rundown storefront. There's no sign, but I already know where we are.

He gets out and stands on the sidewalk, staring up at it.

"Your parents' old bakery?" I ask.

"Yeah," he says softly.

He doesn't say anything else—no doubt he's lost in his memories—so I start snapping photos from different angles.

After that, we take a few shots of the mountains. Then Chase wants one of a sledding hill he said he loved as a child and a few of a maple sugar factory. The town is old and a little run down, but it's so charming. The photos are going to bring the perfect homey touch to his shop in New Haven.

"I think we have enough for now," he says, pulling into the market. "Time to get some ingredients for dinner."

"I agree. I'm definitely working up an appetite."

After he parks, he turns to look at me. "You stay here."

"What? Why?"

"Because I don't want you to see what I'm getting. I want dinner to be a surprise."

I laugh. "I'm not much of a cook. I doubt I'd know what you're making just by looking at an ingredient list."

"Please?" he asks, raising a brow.

"Fiiine," I say, sitting back in my seat and crossing my arms teasingly.

"Thanks. I won't be long."

He heads into the market, and after a few minutes, I get out of the car. The way the snow is sitting on the roof of the market looks pretty cool, so I end up snapping a few photos. Then I turn around and spot a small lake, so I head over to it to take some more shots. Before I know it, twenty minutes have passed, and I start to wonder where Chase is.

Just as the question pops into my head, I see him outside the market with his hands full of bags, talking to some girl.

I start heading his way, unsure if I should approach. But when he spots me, he gets a strange look on his face, so I make the decision to walk over.

"Hey," I say, looking between him and the girl.

"Hey," Chase says, his tone an octave higher than normal. "This is Harper. Harper, this is Birdie."

Harper ... Harper ... why does that sound familiar?

Chase gives me the eye, and then it clicks. Oh, my God! This is her! The girl who told him he was a bad kisser.

I look at her more fully, and notice that she's giving me the eye too. When she looks back at Chase, I can see the hearts in her eyes, so I make a split-second decision.

Wrapping my arm around Chase, I lean into him. He stiffens, but only for a second. Then it's like our bodies click together, like we've put our arms around one another a million times. "Nice to meet you, Harper."

"Likewise," she says, eyeing my arm around his waist. "Chase, I didn't realize you had a girlfriend. You never dated anyone else after me, so I always thought I was your one and only." She says it in a teasing voice, but it comes off so desperate I almost laugh.

"Oh, that's where I heard your name before," I say, snapping the fingers of my free hand. "Chase's middle-school girlfriend." I make a noise between my teeth. "The one who broke up with him on his birthday and told him he was a bad kisser."

Harper sputters, shaking her head. "We all do things we regret when we're young."

"I know," I say. "Most of us don't have kissing experience when we're younger either." I lean further into Chase and give him a heated look. Then I pat him on the chest and turn back to her conspiratorially. "That changes though, and let me tell you, Chase has gotten very, very good with his mouth."

Chase's eyes widen, and Harper's narrow. "How nice," she says, backing away. "Chase, it was good to see you. If you're ever around—"

"We live together in Connecticut now. He won't be around." I wave goodbye, then start pulling Chase toward my car. Once we're out of earshot, we both start laughing.

"I can't believe you just did that," he says, looking at me. "Thank you. I mean, I stopped caring about her a long time ago, but still, it was nice to see that look on her face."

"Are you kidding? I always had dreams of punching that girl. I let her off easy."

He stares at me for a second, then smiles. "You," he says.

"Me what?"

"Nothing, just you."

He puts the groceries in the trunk, then once we're seated in the car, I turn to him. "You had like seven bags and we're two people. What on earth are you making?"

"I told you, it's a surprise."

"Give me one hint."

He pauses, his eyes narrowing as if thinking it over. "Okay, I will. But in return, I get to ask a favor later tonight."

I raise a brow. "What kind of favor?"

"I don't know yet," he says. "Gotta think about it."

"Hmm." I tap my chin, mulling it over. A favor doesn't sound so bad. Chase is a gentleman and a really nice guy, so I know that it won't be anything too crazy. "Deal. A hint for a favor."

He smiles over at me. "Great. Well, I'm cooking us a five-course Christmas-themed dinner. Starting with an appetizer of cranberry and brie bites."

I suck in a breath. "Oh, my God, seriously? Five courses?"

"Maybe more. I'm going to make the most of that kitchen."

I smile, leaning back in my seat. "Wow, okay. That sounds amazing."

"I hope so," he says, grinning back at me.

When we get back to Mistletoe Cabin, we go our separate ways to get ready for dinner. I hum a Christmas tune in the shower, excited for a night with Chase. As friends, of course, I remind myself.

Remembering that I can't cross that line with him is hard. But I think I've been doing a good job of it so far, and

I'm sure it will only get easier from here. The desensitization plan has got to be working by now.

Or maybe I just think our night together will be easy because I had such a good day, and got lucky with my holiday contest photo. Or maybe it's the space from my real life that's helped me feel optimistic. Speaking of, I look at my phone before going downstairs and see multiple missed calls from Rhett, Dasha, and Janice.

But I don't want to talk to any of them at the moment. I want to enjoy my time here before I have to go back to reality tomorrow.

After throwing on a pair of jeans and a blouse, I head downstairs to the great room barefoot. The smells wafting from the kitchen are out of this world, and my stomach growls as I start laying the logs for the fire.

Memories assault me as I stoke the flames to life. Memories of my dad making a fire on Christmas Eve while telling me about the hidden magic in the woods fill my head and the smells of the fire surround me.

I look around the room, deciding then and there that I'm going to bring the tradition of Mistletoe Cabin at Christmas back to life. I'm sure my mom will be on board once I tell her about it. I quickly take out my phone and book next year, and the year after.

Chase enters the room twenty minutes later, carrying a glass of wine. He's in a T-shirt that reads *Cut to the Chase* and underneath is a set of cooking knives.

"Nice T-shirt," I giggle. "Very clever."

He looks down and smiles. "Thanks. Steve Towers, the guy who made it, is around our age. His company started small like mine but now he's global. Gives me hope for the future, you know?"

"You're going to be a success, Chase. I know it."

"Thanks," he says, then holds out the glass of wine. "For you."

"Aren't you going to join me?"

"I have to finish dinner," he tells me, backing away. "But I'll join you for your second glass."

He leaves the room and I settle onto the couch with my wine. Then, for the next half hour or so, I stare into the fire, letting my mind both wander and relax. Ahh, this is exactly what I needed. My mind goes to Chase in the kitchen, and I close my eyes, picturing him working hard behind a hot stove. In my mind he's shirtless, and I groan a little under my breath at the image.

"Birdie?"

I jump to attention. Chase is standing above me with a small smile on his face.

"What were you thinking about just now?" he asks. "I called your name like three times."

"Nothing," I say, blushing. "Just dozed off for a second, I guess."

"Dinner's ready," he says.

He grabs my hand and leads me to the kitchen. When I step inside, I'm instantly dazzled. The island is full of all different types of colorful trays, and the table off to the side is set with plates, a few bowls, and two lit candles.

"Chase, this is too much," I say under my breath. "You didn't have to do all this."

"I wanted to," he says. "Don't think too much into it. This is fun for me, you know?"

I smile at him and try to do as he says. This is honestly the most romantic thing anyone has ever done for me, so it's shocking that the gesture came from a friend.

"I'm sure it's going to be fun for me too," I say honestly.

He hands me another glass of wine, and this time, pours one for himself.

"To our second Christmas together," he says, tapping his glass against mine. "Cheers."

"Cheers," I say, smiling.

"Now," he says. "Let me show you what we're having."

If my mind was blown before, it's nothing compared to when I hear the menu. Along with the cranberry and brie bites, there's cheddar biscuits and roasted brussels sprouts, followed by a holiday apple salad and cauliflower soup. Then there's a baked ham with brown sugar glaze and roasted red potatoes as a main, followed by a red velvet cookie for dessert.

I sit down, practically drooling. "Chase, I can honestly say this will be the best meal of my life."

"Don't say that until you try it," he teases.

I take a bite of a cheddar biscuit, closing my eyes at the delicious flavor. "How did you do all this in such a short amount of time?"

"It's not as hard as it looks once you know what you're doing," he responds.

"Mmhmm," I say, mouth full.

After a few bites of the salad and several spoonfuls of soup, I look up at him in awe. "Everything is delicious. And even if the rest isn't any good, this will still be the best meal this kitchen has ever seen."

He laughs and digs into his own meal, and we entertain ourselves with an easygoing and light conversation about where he learned to cook, and his favorite dishes to make. By the time we're done with the meal, I don't think I can fit another bite. But somehow when he brings out the dessert, I find the room.

I practically have to roll to the living room, and once I

get there, I flop onto the couch. "Thank you," I say. "Whatever favor you're going to ask me is going to be completely worth it. I feel like the surprise element made that meal ten times better."

Chase smiles and sits down by the fire, gesturing to the TV. "So what should we watch?" he asks. "'A Christmas Carol'? 'Santa Claus'? 'Die Hard'?"

I stop scrolling and turn to him. "Did you just say 'Die Hard'?"

"Yeah. Why?"

I give him a look. "That's not a Christmas movie."

"Of course it is."

"No, it is not." I give him a serious look. "Not even close."

He barks out a laugh. "Okay, well, what do you think we should watch, then?"

"'Harry Potter and the Sorcerer's Stone.'"

His jaw drops. "How is *that* a Christmas movie?!"

"It's more of a Christmas movie than 'Die Hard'!"

"No way!"

We go back and forth on this for ten minutes. We start on opposite ends of the large wraparound couch, but by the time we're done debating, we're head to head and inches away in the middle.

"Fine," I say giggling, sinking back on the comfortable cushion. "Let's play it safe with the best Christmas movie of all time ..."

I pause and look over. Then at the same time—

"'Home Alone.'"

We both laugh. "Okay, at least we can agree on that," I say, scrolling to find it.

"Wait. Popcorn," Chase says, jumping up.

"What?! I can't eat another bite."

"You'll have room for this kind of popcorn. Trust me."

He disappears into the kitchen, then comes back with a bowl.

"I'm going to guess that's not Pop Secret," I say wryly.

"Then you'd be right." He chuckles. "I call this Christmas Crunch. It has vanilla candy melts, pretzels, and a little caramel drizzle and red sugar sprinkles."

I shake my head and grab a few kernels. "I could get used to this, you know."

He just smiles in response, so I start the movie.

We settle in, eating popcorn and providing commentary. We make fun of the parts that don't make sense, and smile at the impossibility of the plot. Chase does a marvelous impression of Johnny from the "Angels with Filthy Souls" segment and it makes me laugh until I can't breathe.

But I must have been tired, because I doze off right before the wet bandits break into the house. And when I wake up, there's a black and white movie is playing on the screen. "Miracle on 34th Street," I think.

I turn my head, and spot Chase. He's leaning back on the couch, watching me. Maybe I should feel self-conscious that someone was watching me sleep, but for some reason, it doesn't bother me. It kind of makes me feel safe, like he was watching over me.

"Sorry," I whisper. "I didn't mean to fall asleep."

"It's okay," he says, his voice low.

I watch for a moment as shadows from the dying fire play across his face. I have the strangest desire to reach out and stroke his cheek, but I don't, knowing that wouldn't be a smart move.

I'm just about to excuse myself and go up to bed, when his voice stops me. "I'd like to ask for my favor now."

I press my lips together. "Okay."

He pauses for a moment. "Can I hold you?"

I blink at him, unsure of what that means.

"Please?" he asks. "Just for a little while. I won't do anything inappropriate. But let me pretend, for just a second."

He brings his arm up and over the couch, inviting me to come snuggle in. I hesitate, unsure of how smart it would be to let myself curl up against him. I don't *technically* have a boyfriend, so it would be okay, right?

And when I see that curved smile on his face, I can't resist.

Smiling back, I nod. "Okay."

I cross the distance between us and then cuddle into the crook of his arm. Taking a deep breath, I snuggle in and rest my cheek on his chest. He's so warm, and he smells like Christmas morning. His arm drops down around me and the tips of his fingers land on my waist.

I'm just about to close my eyes when he suddenly leans over. "Your tattoo ... is that a ..."

I nod, then reach over and pull the side of my blouse up so he can see. "Yeah. It's a snowflake."

I don't have to explain why I got the snowflake, and Chase doesn't need to ask. His chest rises and falls with a large breath, and for a brief moment, I feel a barely-there touch on the tattoo. I smile, somehow happy that he's now seen the tattoo I got in his honor.

My eyes then close of their own accord, and I'm unable to remember the last time I was this comfortable.

His cheek comes down to rest against the top of mine, and for a second, I pretend just like he does.

Then just before I drift off to sleep, I feel his lips press gently against my forehead.

22

I wake up in the master bedroom just as light starts spilling through the window.

I have a brief memory of Chase carrying me to my room in the wee hours of the morning, but the last thing I really remember is being in his arms. He held me for hours while I dozed on and off, while an endless stream of Christmas movies played in the background.

It felt good to be held by him. Too good. I don't know if cuddling with him set me back in my plan or not, but I don't regret it. For a few hours I felt warm, safe ... cared for.

But now it's time to go home and get back to reality, where we both have to face our problems.

I look at my phone, seeing more texts and missed calls from Rhett and Janice. I text them both back and let them know I'll be home by late afternoon, then get out of bed to shower.

By the time I make it downstairs, the smell of breakfast reaches my nose.

"You're spoiling me," I say, walking into the kitchen.

Chase grins and hands me a gingerbread latte. "I

promise this is just as much for me as it is for you. I wanted to use the kitchen one last time before we left."

I scoop some eggs and grab a couple of pancakes. "This looks great. And dinner last night was out of this world."

He smiles, sipping his coffee. "Thanks, I ..."

I wait for him to finish and when he doesn't, I look up.

He shakes his head. "I just wanted to say I had a really good time. Thanks for letting me stay here."

"I had a good time too, Chase."

My phone vibrates on the table between us, and the sound feels like the ding of a stopwatch.

Time's up.

Chase smiles and stands. "I'll bring our bags to the car. We should try to get an early start."

I nod. "Okay. I'll clean up here and check out."

He gives me one last lingering look, then disappears from the kitchen.

Once we're packed up and ready to go, I look up at the house once more, excited for next year when I get to come back on Christmas.

Our drive back is pretty uneventful. The weather is nice, and Chase and I keep the conversation light. He tells me a little bit more about his family, and I talk about the business Dasha and I want to start. He's so interested in what I do, and I can't help but wish that Rhett would ask me the questions that Chase does.

As soon as Rhett comes to mind, I start to feel guilty because I haven't spent much time thinking about him this weekend. My thoughts were either on Chase, my dad, or the holiday photo contest.

In his latest text, Rhett told me that he would be studying in the library until later tonight, but he wanted to get a late dinner together. I agreed, because we do have to talk things out. I don't know where we'll go from here, but we can't go on like we have been, without speaking.

When I see the sign for New Haven, I turn to Chase, who's scrolling through the photos I took on my camera.

"I just remembered," I tell him. "There are some frames I have that I think would look amazing in your shop. The black ones you had up were fine, but now that I know which photos we took, I think you'd be better off with a white."

He nods. "Sounds good to me. I defer to your judgment here."

"I'll swing by my apartment first so we can grab them."

"Sounds good."

But when we get to my apartment, Rhett is sitting on the stoop, his eyes on my car. My stomach sinks as I pull to a slow stop.

"Shit," I say under my breath. "He's supposed to be at the library."

"I'm guessing he doesn't know I went on this trip with you."

"Of course not," I say, looking at Chase. "I didn't tell anyone."

Chase nods, but I can tell he's a little hurt that I kept him a secret. But he can't really blame me, can he? What did he expect? I don't have the time to get those answers now, however, because Rhett is by my driver's side window, his eyes on Chase. I force a smile and get out of the car. "Rhett, hey."

Rhett's eyes flick to Chase who's getting out on the other side. "Chase? What are you doing here?" He looks back at me. "What's going on?"

My mind races for an excuse. Luckily, I can give him a little bit of the truth. "I called Chase because I wanted to show him some of the photos I took for the shop."

Rhett stares at me. "Photos for the shop?"

I smack my forehead. "Oh, I didn't tell you? When we did the tasting, I offered to take some photos for him to fill the frames on the exposed wall. He's from Vermont, so I thought it would be a good idea to get some scenery shots of his home state while I was up there. You know, to make the space more personal and homier."

"Oh," Rhett responds. "Good idea, I guess."

I can tell Rhett believes me, but I can also sense that he's not thrilled about the situation. When he turns to Chase, his smile seems forced. "You should have talked to me about this first. As your investor I need to be included—or at least informed—of these decisions."

The frustration on Chase's face is obvious—at least to me. "I didn't think giving Birdie the opportunity to showcase her work would be an issue. From what I've seen so far, she's incredibly talented. Figured it would be fine to go ahead."

"She is talented," Rhett agrees immediately. "And it is fine. I just want to be kept in the loop, that's all. It's my money that's on the line here."

Chase's lips thin, but he nods. The tension between the three of us is growing by the second, and I curse myself for being the cause of this situation once again. I'm letting my selfishness get in the way of things that are much more important. I think about Chase's family and all the weight he's carrying on his shoulders, and the guilt I feel grows to crushing levels.

"I'd better drop him off home," I say, wanting to diffuse the situation. "I'll see you—"

"Wait—" Rhett says, his voice dropping. "I need to talk to you."

"Now?" I sneak a glance at Chase, who is now looking down at his phone.

"Yes. Because I've been wanting to apologize since our fight, and I can't wait any longer." He takes my hands in his. "I'm sorry, Birdie. We can forget the whole California thing. I don't know if I'll ever have an opportunity like that again, but I love you, and what you want is more important to me. We don't have to move there."

I tense, annoyed with his half apology. I'm just about to pull away, when he squeezes my hands. "I mean it. I don't know what I'd do without you."

The look in his eye is familiar to me. He's scared. He's scared that I'm going to leave him. I stare at him, feeling guilty. Fear will always will be my trigger. I never want to hurt anyone I love by leaving them. How could I knowingly bring that pain into someone's life when I know what it feels like? I can't do it. I can't.

Then I think of Chase, and realize that even though it's inadvertent, I've been hurting him too. I've been leading him on, which is unfair, especially because he deserves better. He has so much on his plate already, and I'm just adding to his load. How could I be so selfish?

I make the decision then and there to make my position clear. Something inside me is telling me I'm a coward, but I tamp that voice down and smile at Rhett.

And when he leans down to kiss me, I let him. His mouth is more fervent than usual, and his hands on my butt proprietary, but I let it go on all the same. I'm with Rhett. I've been with him forever. All my thoughts and fantasies about Chase have to come to an end, especially for his sake.

Chase must take the hint, because when I surface from the kiss a few moments later, he's gone.

23

I'm at my mother's for our annual cookie-baking night. Usually, I enjoy this time with her. But this year, I'm distracted.

I haven't heard from Chase all week. I didn't expect to, but after all the time we spent together in the car and in Vermont, it feels weird to have no contact. I miss him, but I haven't changed my mind about my decision to choose Rhett. Despite the emotions Chase brings out in me, and despite the intensity of our connection, I can't just turn my life upside down because he's made a sudden reappearance.

Things with Rhett have been better since our break. He hasn't brought up California again, but I sense it there, hovering between us. It's like a small thorn in both of our sides. It can be ignored for a little while, but not forever.

Am I being unfair to deny Rhett this opportunity? This is a chance of a lifetime for him, but I just can't see myself making a move to the West Coast. Is it really right for me to hold him back?

Janice thinks I'm crazy for not going, and even Dasha

told me that if that's what I wanted to do, we could still make our business work.

But I don't want to do it, and if I'm being honest with myself, I know why. My dad isn't on the West Coast. I have no memories of him there, and that scares me. Not to mention I could never move so far from my mother. She's all I've got. And she'd be alone without me.

The ding of the timer snaps me out of my reverie, but my mom gets up before I can. "First batch is ready!" she singsongs on her way to the stove. "Pour me a little more mulled wine, will you? Nothing like a sugar cookie and a spicy drink."

I laugh and ladle some more of the hot liquid into her mug, shaking off my bad mood. My mom started this tradition as something that she and I could do together, just us. My dad would always bring home cookies and treats from all over the world, but my mom said there was something special about baking them yourself. Now that I've spent many cozy Christmases baking cookies with her, I agree.

A few minutes later, she comes back with a tray of cookies. "Careful, they're hot," she says, sitting beside me.

I grab a cookie and take a bite, closing my eyes as the sweetness washes over my tongue. It doesn't to compare to anything Chase would make, but the flavor reminds me of home. Sometimes there's just no beating that.

"Now that you've got a little sugar in you, why don't you tell me what's on your mind?"

I hesitate. I haven't told anyone about Chase and Vermont, but I realize now that I have to get it off my chest.

"Don't judge me," I say, giving her a look.

"I would never," she vows, looking worried. "Did something happen? Are you okay?"

I rub my hand over my face. "I'm fine. But yes, something did happen."

I go on to tell her all about the past weekend. I tell her everything from my fight with Rhett, to Candy Cane, to taking photos at Chase's old shop and then falling asleep in his arms.

She listens intently, and when I'm done, pulls me into a hug.

"Oh, Birdie," she says. "It's okay to be confused. You're young."

"I just wish I didn't think about him so much," I reveal. "I made my decision to stay with Rhett, and I'm going to stick to it. But no matter how hard I try, I can't erase Chase from my brain. Can you help me? How do I do that?"

My mom makes a noise. "I'm not sure anyone can completely erase the memory of someone else, sweetheart. We know that better than anyone." She smooths my hair with her hand. "I'll tell you what you can do, though. Why don't you tell Chase how you feel? And Rhett too?"

"I've tried that, but I can never find the words. It's like whenever I go to open my mouth, I completely freeze. Sometimes I feel like everything is trapped inside me, buried way down deep. I've been like that since I was little."

"Maybe I can help." My mom stares at me, then gets up. "Be right back," she says.

When she returns, she sits down next to me and drops a photo album in front of us. I recognize it as our Christmas album and smile. "Feeling nostalgic, Mom?"

"Something like that."

I open the album and run my hand down the first page. "I love this picture of you two."

The photo is of my mom and dad by the tree during

their first Christmas together. My mom is pregnant and my dad looks so happy. He's got both his hands on her belly.

"I love it too," my mom says softly. "It was before your dad got famous. Things were easier back then."

"Easier?" I laugh. "You guys were fresh out of college with no jobs and dealing with a surprise pregnancy."

She shakes her head. "Surprise is an understatement. We'd only been dating two months when I found out."

I nudge her shoulder. "Yeah, but now you have me."

"And I don't regret it for a second."

I turn the page and go through a few more photos. Me on my first Christmas wearing a Santa hat. Me as a toddler surrounded by porcelain dolls and then again at age seven on a pink bike. There are so many good memories. That's why when I look up, I'm surprised to see my mom frowning.

"Mom? What is it?"

She looks fidgety. And when her eyes meet mine, and it's obvious she has something to tell me.

"I brought this album out for another reason," she says. "Because I think it's time I was honest about something."

"Okay ..." I lean back in my chair, nervous. I've never seen her like this.

She runs a hand over a photo of my father standing in front of Mistletoe Cabin. "Your father was a great man. He had a personality that was larger than life and he was an incredible father. Watching him with you was and always will be one of the greatest joys of my life."

I already don't like where this is going. "Is there a but coming?"

"I loved him. But ... I wasn't *in love* with him. Not the way I should have been. And because you're an adult now, and because I think I can be honest with you, the truth is I was in love with someone else."

Time slows down, and a terrible flush runs up and over my arms. "Mom, what are you talking about?"

She blinks away tears. "I'm sorry, but it's the truth."

I push back from the table, needing space from her. "I don't understand what you're telling me. You and Dad were in love. I saw you together with my own eyes. Why are you even telling me this?"

"Your dad was in love with his art. That always came first."

"*We* came first! He was always there for us!"

"Of course he was. I'm not saying he wasn't. I'm just telling you how I felt back then."

Spots of angry red flash across my line of vision. "Did Dad know this? That you weren't in love with him?"

"I doubt it," she responds, looking sad. "He never slowed down enough to notice."

"You're blaming him? I can't believe this." I get up and start pacing. "Why did you stay with him? And don't say it's because of me."

"It wasn't only because of you. I was scared to leave him. Who would leave the great Roy Tenneson? I was a coward, and I couldn't get myself to do it." She looks up at me, her eyes pleading. "I wasn't unhappy. I loved your father, Birdie. Don't get me wrong. We had a nice life. But ... I shouldn't have stayed. I should have followed my heart and been with the person I was truly in love with, even if that would have been a more difficult path. Do you understand?"

"No, I don't understand. And I don't understand why you're telling me this now. Are you trying to ruin all of my childhood memories a week before Christmas?"

"Our memories can never be ruined. Everything about them was real."

I throw my hands up. "Then why tell me?"

"Because I don't want you to make the same mistake as me."

Her words lash me like a whip. "What's that supposed to mean?"

She walks up to me and puts both hands on my shoulders. "Are you sure Rhett is what you want? That's you're completely, one hundred percent in love with him? Are you absolutely sure?"

I pull away from her. "My relationship has nothing to do with yours. Why even bring him up?"

"Because I want you to be happy, Birdie. I don't want you to stay with someone you're not completely sure about because you think it's the right thing to do. I don't want you to do what I did."

"I would never do what you did," I snap, grabbing my purse. "Dad deserved better."

"He did. But so did I."

I head for the door, not bothering to turn back. "Great night, Mom. Thanks for letting me know my entire life has been a lie."

She says something else, but I slam the door too loud to hear her.

When I get back to the apartment, Rhett takes one look at my face and comes rushing forward. "Birdie? What happened?"

"It's my mom ..."

"Your mom?" He walks me over the couch and sits me down. "Is she okay?"

I tell him everything that she told me—except for the part about him. Just saying it out loud makes it feel horribly real, and the little girl in me doesn't want to believe it. My family has always been sacred to me, and I don't know if I can ever forgive my mother for ruining my memories.

"Wow," Rhett says, shaking his head. "That's tough ..."

The way he says it has me looking up. "But?"

He shrugs. "I don't know. I mean, don't get mad at me for saying so, but is it really that big of a deal? She said she loved him, but she just wasn't *obsessed* with him. I mean, everyone else was, so it's not like he lived some sad, lonely life."

"I just ... always thought they were happy."

But now that I look back on some of the things my mom has said and done over the years, it all starts to make sense. The two of them couldn't have been more opposite. My mom is a quiet homebody, and my dad was an eccentric extrovert. He loved grand Christmases in Vermont, while my mom likes simple baking nights at home in her little kitchen.

Still, she lied to him, and she lied to me.

"She said they were still happy," Rhett says. "And let's face it, everyone settles a little bit on certain things, you know what I mean?"

"Love shouldn't be one of them."

He smiles and pecks my lips. "My little romantic. One of the reasons I love you."

"I love you, too."

The automatic words, however, feel hollow and wooden coming off my tongue—especially after everything my mom and I talked about.

"Tell you what," he says. "How about I take you out tomorrow night? We can go to your little Christmas town, or whatever."

I stare at him, surprised. "Really? You hate it there."

"I know, but you don't. And I want to do what I can to cheer you up. You had a tough week. First the stress of the holiday photo contest, and now everything with your mom."

"I'd love that, thanks."

But the mention of the holiday contest has my mood plummeting. The day after I got back from Vermont, I pulled up the photo series I took of the moose. I was so excited to edit and submit it. But when I had it in front of me on my computer, it didn't feel perfect like it did when I took the photos.

My father loved moose. They were one of his favorite animals and subjects to paint. And I think that's what the problem was. The picture felt perfect for my father, but not for me.

If I end up with nothing else, I'll submit the moose picture, but I'm hoping I can find something that works with the little time I have left before the deadline.

Maybe tomorrow my luck will turn around.

24

———

"You're in a good mood," I say, looking over at Rhett. "I know you're just coming here as a favor to me, but if I didn't know any better, I'd say you're looking forward to this."

"Must be holiday spirit," he says, winking at me.

He pulls into a parking garage near the Christmas tree, and once we find a space, I start getting my camera ready. I look up, sending a silent message to the world that I'll find a photo here today. I get out of the car, feeling a little bit more reenergized.

"Why don't you take a picture of us?" Rhett suggests as we start walking toward the main street. "Maybe by the tree?"

I shake my head. "No offense, but I don't want to turn in anything staged. And portraits aren't really my thing. I'd like to submit a scenery shot or ..."

I trail off when I realize Rhett isn't listening to me. He's typing furiously on his phone, his brow furrowed. I sigh, falling into step beside him.

"Let's go to the tree anyway," he suggests a few minutes later.

Before I can say anything, he grabs my hand and starts pulling me toward the square.

A knot forms in the center of my stomach. He's acting strange, and I can't help but wonder what's going on with him. It crosses my mind that he might be proposing, but I instantly dismiss the idea. He would never choose a random date, let alone somewhere he hates that doesn't live up to his usual level of fanfare. But if it's not that, then what could it be? Nervous, I drag my feet, but it does nothing to slow him down.

It's been a long time since I've come here at night, and while the tree looks spectacular, my heart is slowly climbing into my throat. I try to focus on the thousands of tiny lights decorating the massive pine, but all it does is make me feel dizzy.

"Rhett, can you slow down?" I ask. "What's the rush?"

He suddenly stops and points across the square. "Hey, look. Isn't that Janice and Chase?"

Wait ... what? Hearing their two names together sends my pulse into a sickening gallop. And when I follow Rhett's gloved finger and spot the two of them together, I sway on the spot.

"They can't be on a date," I say without thinking.

And it doesn't look like they are. Not exactly, anyway. They aren't holding hands or mooning over each other, but why else would they be together?

"Why can't they?" Rhett asks, a bite in his tone. "They make sense as a couple. Their families are both working class, and they're used to a simpler lifestyle than we are. You know what I mean."

His comment has me stiffening, because I know exactly

what he means by that. They're not from money like Rhett and me, and therefore of course they'd make a good couple. But any anger at Rhett dissipates and gets directed toward the couple walking toward us. Janice has looped her arm though Chase's, and the smile on her face tells me she knows exactly what she's doing and how it will affect me.

I remind myself quickly that I don't have any right to get upset. I'm dating Rhett, and I have no hold on Chase. But still, it just doesn't make sense. Janice has no interest in Chase, at least that's what she told me. So why else would she be doing this to me?

"Hey, guys! What are you doing here?" Janice asks as they approach.

I stare at Chase, willing him to look at me, but he doesn't budge. "Just here to take some photos for the holiday contest," I finally reply, turning my gaze to her.

That gets Chase looking in my direction. He's probably confused. He thinks I took the photo back in Vermont.

"Fun," Janice says. "Chase and I were just at the bakery. I asked him to teach me a little bit about desserts and what he does."

She nudges him and gives him a secret smile, indicating that's not all they're doing. Anger and jealousy war viciously inside me. "Since when are you interested in sweets? I had to beg you to come to the tasting." I say, annoyed.

Her eyes narrow ever so slightly. "It's the holidays. Nothing wrong with a little indulgence here and there."

Such bullshit. I almost call her out on it, but I don't want to stoop to her level.

"Ain't that the truth," Rhett says, throwing an arm around me. "Speaking of, are you guys hungry? Birdie and I were going to grab a bite to eat first."

"We'd love to join you," Janice says, grinning up at him.

"How about the Snow Café? They're serving these cute little Christmas tapas you'd just love, Birdie."

Eating with them is the last thing I want to do, but apparently, it's not up to me. Rhett starts steering us toward the end of the street before I can have any say in the matter.

"We'd love to," he says over his shoulder.

He keeps his arm around me the whole walk there, and it's all I can do to not throw it off. I don't understand what's happening right now. Why are Janice and Chase really together? The thought of the two of them being on an actual date has me seeing red, and I almost make the excuse that I'm not feeling well and have to leave.

But I don't want to let either of them know I'm as affected as I am. Besides, Chase and Janice have every right to be out on a date, if that's what this is, and I'm not going to say anything else about it.

Once we get to the restaurant, we're seated at a four-top by the window. I'm across from Janice, and she wastes no time starting up a conversation with me and pretending like everything is okay.

"Look at this," she says, pointing to the menu. "Bacon-wrapped water chestnuts and roasted parmesan garlic shrimp. I told you you'd like it here."

"Mmm," I respond, unable to manage anything else. Right now, they could be serving the Last Supper and I wouldn't care.

Before I look down at the menu, I catch a look exchanged between Rhett and Janice that has the red flags in my stomach waving. What was that all about? What am I missing here?

"Chase," Rhett says. "Maybe take a look at the dessert menu. No time like the present to come up with a few more options."

Chase nods, as if he too is lost for words. I have a feeling he didn't expect to end up on a double date with Rhett and me either. He looks more tense than I've ever seen him, and more and more, I start to wonder if something else is at play here.

Janice suddenly leans over against Chase to point something out, her boobs conspicuously on display and touching his arm.

"Janice," I start, the red I'm seeing starting to blind me. "Did you bring your medicine?"

"What medicine?" she asks.

"You know, for your lactose intolerance. You know it flares up when you have dessert."

Her lips thin. "No, I didn't. I haven't had an issue in a while. I'm perfectly fine."

"Oh, that's right." A part of me regrets blowing her spot up, but I can't help it. After being under attack for so long, a person will eventually go on the defense.

"So," Janice says, a sugary-sweet smile on her face. "Any news on the California front? Did you guys make a decision?"

Rhett stiffens and so do I. The California matter is still hovering there between us like a bad smell. From the look on Janice's face, I'd suspect she knows that and is looking to cause trouble.

"Even though it's a once-in-a-lifetime opportunity," Rhett starts before turning to me with a smile that I don't quite believe, "we've decided not to take it."

Janice sucks her teeth. "That's too bad. I'd kill to move out west. Get away from all this cold and snow."

"Right?!" Rhett says. "There's no downsides to Cali, in my opinion."

"There are in mine," I snap, feeling ganged up on. "And I like the cold and snow."

"But what about late-night walks on the beach and drinks under the sun?" Janice rests her chin in her hand. "Sounds like a dream."

"We'd be smack in the middle of L.A. too—right where all the action happens," Rhett continues.

"You'd probably see so many celebrities," Janice gushes.

"I know. It would be the best—"

"We're not moving to California!" I shout a little too loudly.

Everyone at the table quiets, and a few other customers turn to look in my direction. I regret my outburst, but I've had enough. Between the news from my mother, everything with Rhett, and now Chase and Janice, I just can't deal.

"Excuse me," I say, slamming my napkin down on my plate.

"Birdie, come on. Of course we're not moving, I was just imagining what it would be like," Rhett says.

"It's fine," I lie, shoving my seat back. "I'm just tired and need some air. It's been a long week."

I hurry away from the table and head for the back of the café. There's a smoker's deck outside, and even though it's cold—and I don't smoke—I settle into one of the seats and put my head in my hands.

Everything is so confusing lately. My relationship with my mother, my relationship with Rhett, my friendship with Janice—why can't I get a handle on my life? It's not Chase's fault, but since his arrival, it's like I just can't seem to figure anything out or make the right decisions. I can't even tell anyone how I feel for fear of what their reactions will be. I seem to be burying myself deeper and deeper into a hole that I had no idea I was going to fall into.

I wish I could sit around and sulk for the rest of the night, but I know I have to go back. I'll have to pretend that Janice and Chase sitting next to each other means nothing to me, and apologize to Rhett for storming off. As for my mother, I'll deal with her later.

Forcing some semblance of calm, I make my way back into the restaurant.

But all that calm goes out the window when I see that Chase is in the hallway waiting for me.

"Are you okay?" he asks softly.

"What are you doing back here?" I look around. "You should leave. They'll get suspicious."

"I don't care what they think."

My lips thin. "Oh? But what about Janice? That's not a nice thing to say about your *date*."

"It's not a date." He scrubs a hand over his face, then leans back against the wall. "She asked for my help and I was going to say no because it sounded like bullshit, but then she mentioned there was a chance you were going to be here." He looks away, shaking his head. "I know it's dumb, but I just wanted to see you. It's been a while."

"Oh."

His eyes meet mine. "I didn't know that this was one of her catty games. I'm sorry."

So Janice knew I would be coming here. Things start falling together, and I realize that she and Rhett must have planned this somehow. But why?

"It's okay. It's not your fault."

He nods, then leans against the wall, his eyes still on mine. "Vermont seems like a dream I made up in my head. That time with you? It was everything to me. And now seeing you with him … it sucks. It just really sucks."

"I know it does. It sucks for me too. But I can't keep having this conversation with you, Chase. It's too hard."

"Then stop fighting it," he says suddenly, his eyes flashing. "Stop fighting this."

I shake my head, flustered. "No, we've been over this."

He takes a step toward me, and the heat from his body warms me from head to toe. I so badly want to lean into him, to soak him up, but I can't. I just can't. "Chase …"

"Choose me, Birdie," he whispers, gently grasping my fingertips with his own.

I look up and meet his eyes. His are locked on mine, a fierceness in them I've never seen before. "Pick me," he says. "Choose me. I want you more than he does, and I'm better for you. I swear to you, we're better together."

His words wash over me, and I find I'm unable to look away. The intensity between us sparks red and bright, and for a moment, I let myself bask in it. I stop time and live in the moment with him, like I've been dying to do from the beginning. I've never felt anything like it, and I don't know that I ever will again.

I know that he's locked in this moment with me too, and when I feel the tips of his fingers on my cheeks, I pull in a slow breath. Just this simple touch feels so good, even though the gentle caress is a stark contrast to the torment going on inside me.

"I want you so bad," he tells me, scanning my face. "I need you more than I've ever needed anything. I—"

"Birdie? Chase?"

And just like that, our bubble bursts once again. Janice's voice reaches us from down the hall, and we both jump back—Chase a little more reluctantly.

When she comes to stand beside us, I glare at her. "What do you want?"

She holds up two hands. "I just came to see if you were all right. When you didn't come back to the table, I was worried."

I scoff, wanting to say so many things. I want to tell her that she's been a horrible friend, and that I have no idea what I did to deserve this treatment. Then I want to tell her I'm worried about her, because if she's acting this way, there must be something really wrong. I want to rant and rave and yell at her for whatever scheming she's done with Rhett and lay into her for involving Chase, but I don't. I just stand there like the coward I am.

"I'm fine," I eventually get out. "I just needed some air. Then I ran into Chase here on my way back. Anyway, meet you both back at the table."

Without waiting for an answer, or looking at Chase again, I sidestep them both and disappear down the hall.

25

"Okay, what's going on?" Dasha asks, turning toward me in the dressing room. "That's the third call you've silenced since we got here."

Little does she know I've only been accepting calls from her. Ever since the failed cookie-baking night and the disastrous double date a few days ago, I haven't been talking to anyone.

After I returned to the table that night in Christmas town, I told Rhett I had a headache and we went home. I couldn't be there another minute. Not with the tension between Chase and me. Just remembering his words —"Choose me, pick me ..."—sends an unwanted but pleasurable thrill through me. It's so tempting, but I just can't upend my life for him—not when it's already going down in flames.

I also left because I didn't want to spend another moment in Janice's company, not after what she did. I thought about confronting Rhett on the ride home about the way he'd schemed with her, but decided it wasn't even worth it. Whatever their reasoning was for doing what they did wouldn't be good enough for me anyway.

"I just want to pick out dresses in peace," I say, which is a half-truth.

"Hmm." Dasha makes a noise and comes to stand beside me. "Your mom called me."

"She did?"

"She wanted to come. She wanted to be here when you pick out *the* dress, as she called it."

I hang up a few gowns I grabbed off the rack, having barely looked at them. "What does that mean? *The* dress? It's just another one of Rhett's Christmas parties."

"You know it's not. He's going to propose to you in that dress."

I stiffen. I was hoping the proposal wouldn't be brought up today. Despite all that's going on between us, Rhett has been dropping hint after hint that he's going to propose at the Christmas party. Rhett has a lot of great qualities, but can I really marry a man who thinks so little of my career? And who always puts himself first? I don't know, and I need more time to figure that out.

I sit down on the bench, unable to hide my anxiety any longer. "I don't think I'm ready to be engaged."

"I don't blame you," Dasha says softly, sitting down beside me. "But if you're not ready, you should tell him."

"I want to. But I can never find the words. They're stuck inside me—completely frozen. Just like me."

It's why I can't tell Rhett how I really feel. It's why I never stand up for myself when it comes to Janice. It's like I'm stuck in a picture I don't remember being taken.

"I wish I could help," Dasha says. "I wish I could—"

A knock on the door startles us both.

"Oh, that must be Janice," Dasha says, jumping to her feet.

I stop her with an arm. "Janice? What is she doing here?"

Dasha cocks her head to the side, clearly confused. "What do you mean? She always shops with us for Rhett's parties." Her face falls. "Wait, did you not invite her on purpose?"

I look away. "It's my own fault. I didn't tell you."

"Oh no," she whispers. "I should have known that when she called asking for details, something was wrong. I'm sorry. Do you want me to tell her to go home?"

"No, she's here, so we might as well let her in. Maybe she can tell us why she was on a date with Chase the other night."

Dasha's jaw drops. "Oh, my God. What?"

I walk around her and head for the door. When I open it, Janice is there with a smile on her face. "Sorry I'm late," she says, breezing by me. "What did I miss?"

Dasha is not like me. She says how she feels, and I can tell by her face she isn't going to let Janice get away with coming in here like nothing's wrong. "You didn't miss anything. But apparently I missed a lot."

Janice looks between us. "What are you talking about?"

"Your date with Chase?" Dasha asks, her cheeks turning pink. "How could you do that?"

"Oh, Lord. I should have known," Janice says, rolling her eyes. "First of all, it wasn't a date."

"You were all over him," I say, glaring at her.

"I wasn't all over him any more than I'm all over any guy," Janice says, throwing her hands up. "What's the big deal?"

"What was going on between you and Rhett?" I demand, crossing my arms.

She's quiet for a moment, then she sighs. "If you must know, he's insecure about you and Chase and I don't blame him. Of course he didn't say that to me verbatim, but when he called me up asking if I'd take Chase out, I saw right through it. I told him where we'd be, and he suggested we meet."

"And why would you help him with that? With ... trapping me?" I ask. "Are you trying to get back at me for something I did?"

"No, I'm doing it because I care about you," she says, standing up and walking toward me. "If you haven't noticed, you've been kind of a mess lately."

"Because you care about me?" I laugh loudly. "Bullshit. You've been treating me like dirt."

"I've been trying to save you from making a huge mistake!" she shouts. "Whenever Chase shows up like some fairytale prince, you turn into a total basket case."

"That's not fair," I yell. "You know what that Christmas meant to me. I'm human and—"

"You can't see the nose in front of your face," she hisses. "Don't you think poor Rhett notices how you and Chase stare at each other? Anyone with eyes could see it." She crosses her arms across her chest, giving me a very pointed look. "And you know what? If you think I've been mean, it's only because you've been so thoughtless."

"Thoughtless? How can you say that?!"

"Running off to Vermont with Chase?"

I blink at her, stunned. How did she find out? I didn't tell anyone.

She scoffs and crosses her arms. "Yeah, I know all about that. You should tell lover boy to watch what he puts on social media. He had a picture of Mistletoe Cabin on his

Instagram story. You're lucky Rhett didn't see it. I thought about showing him, but I didn't."

"You thought about showing him?" I stare at her in shock. "What happened to my friend? I thought you were supposed to be on my side. I don't even know who you are right now."

"I'm just here to try to help you accept reality." She walks over to my stack of gowns, flips over the price tag for the dress on top, and laughs. "Something you think you'll never have to do. But looks like not even *you* can have everything."

And with that said, she leaves the dressing room, slamming the door behind her.

26

"Still no luck on the holiday photo, huh?"

I look up at Mr. Donovan and somehow manage a smile. "Am I that obvious?"

He pulls out the chair beside me and sits down. "I have a classroom full of very excited students exchanging submission photos and discussing filters, and one student who's sitting by herself in the corner."

"I do have something," I say, turning over the picture and handing him the photo I took of the moose. "But it doesn't feel right for the contest."

"Why not?"

"It doesn't feel like ... me. It feels more like my dad."

"Ah." He stares at the photo and nods. "Then you're right. This isn't your submission. It can't feel like someone else. It has to feel like you."

"I did what you said," I tell him. "I went to Vermont for inspiration—to a place that's very special to me. It feels like Christmas there, but even that didn't work. I don't know what else to do."

"Hmm," Professor Donovan says. "I think you need to look at things differently, then."

"But how?"

"Can I tell you a story?" he asks, smiling. "About the time I took what I believe is the best picture I've ever taken?"

"Yeah, sure." I need all the help I can get.

"It was many years ago, back when I was eighteen and a student here. There was a girl I was crazy about, but I was too afraid to tell her. You see, she and I were really good friends, and I didn't want ruin that by confessing to her how I felt. But as time went on, I realized that if I didn't say anything, then I'd lose her forever.

"Anyway, I wanted to do something romantic. Something that would blow her away and show her the true depth of my emotions. What better way, of course, than with a picture? I was studying photography back then and thought there must be some way I could use my talent and let her know without words."

"That does sound romantic," I say truthfully. "So what did you do?"

"I took photos of her whenever I could. Some when she was looking, and some when she wasn't. It was my goal to capture every one of her emotions, so she could see herself from my point of view. She was so beautiful to me from moment to moment, and in every moment.

"And then one day right before Christmas, I took a picture of her just as the first snow of the year started to fall. The smile on her face was breathtaking, and I knew then that this picture would say what I couldn't. It was an absolutely perfect candid of this woman at her happiest. But after I snapped the photo and put down the camera ..."

I lean forward, wondering why his words trailed off. "What? What happened?"

He gives me a sad smile. "I put down the camera and saw that she was smiling at someone. That smile wasn't for me, and it wasn't for the snow. It was for someone else."

"Oh," I frown. "I'm so sorry. That must have been hard."

"It was." He laughs. "But I still have that photo, and to me, it's still perfect. I felt that way when I took it. And all these years later, I still feel the same. I captured a moment in time that I never want to forget. You'll know yours when you see it."

"I hope so."

"There is always hope," he says, standing up. "In fact, this woman and I recently reconnected."

A smile breaks across my face. "No way. Really?"

"Really," he says, his eyes light. "So if I didn't give up, then neither should you."

He walks away. His story gave me a little spark, so I spend the rest of class looking at my classmates' submissions and helping them brainstorm ideas. I still don't have an idea myself, but at least now, I have a little hope.

I'm walking out of class when it hits me.

Something about Mr. Donovan's story ...

But it can't be. Can it?

Running on adrenaline, I race to my car. Within a half an hour I'm at my mom's house, and a few seconds later I'm bursting through the door.

"Is it you?" I ask.

She jumps from her spot on the couch, nearly dropping her coffee. "Birdie? What on earth—"

"Is it you in Professor Donovan's story?"

She shakes her head. "What story? Birdie, what's going on?"

"Professor Donovan told me he had a friend back when he was in school that he was in love with. He took dozens of photos of her, and he was going to use them to tell her, but she was in love with someone else. Is he talking about you?"

Her mouth gapes for a second, as if she's searching for words. But then her shoulders relax and she smiles. "Yes. He is."

I sink down onto the couch, shocked. "Wow."

She puts down her coffee and leans forward. "Henry—that is, Professor Donovan—and I were very good friends in college. And unknowingly, we both had feelings for one another."

"But ... then why ..."

I can't finish the sentence, too overwhelmed to go on, but she seems to know what I'm asking. "Because before we did anything about our feelings, I met your father and got swept away by his charm. It was before he was famous, but there was still something so special about him. I don't ever regret my time with him, Birdie. Especially because it gave me you. I want you to know that." She squeezes my hand.

"Henry fell off my radar," she continues, "but as the years went on, I realized what a mistake I made by not telling him how I felt. And by the time I figured out how I felt, it was too late. I already had a family I could never betray."

Closing my eyes, I let her words sink in. A part of me is still so hurt to find out the truth about my parents, but another part is urging me that I have to move on. Because that's just it. The truth is the truth, and I can't run from it.

"I'm sorry," I say. "I shouldn't have gotten so upset the other day."

"Of course you should have," my mom says, coming over to sit beside me. "You're allowed to feel and process big news however you like."

Something else occurs to me. "Wait, Professor Donovan

also told me he and this woman recently reconnected ...”

My mom blushes. She actually blushes. “We have. I reached out a few months ago on a whim, and the rest is history. We've been spending time together at his cabin upstate. That's why I've been a bit unreachable lately. We don't have very good service up there.”

Despite everything else I'm feeling, a small burst of happiness filters through. “That's great, Mom. Professor Donovan seems like a nice guy.”

“He's the best. I only wish I hadn't waited so long to tell him how I felt. I never forgot about him all those years, and things with him are still so ... easy. They feel right, not forced. There's magic between us.”

It's rare my mom uses that word, and it triggers something inside me.

I have to start being honest with myself. Truly honest. I love Rhett, but the magic isn't there. There is definitely something between me and Chase, though. And my body, heart, and soul can no longer ignore it or pretend it doesn't exist.

But just entertaining the thought of being with him means that I have to make some changes and hard decisions. It isn't fair to anyone to go on like I have been.

“I have to end things with Rhett,” I suddenly say to my mom.

The words hurt coming out.

Fear is running rampant through me.

But I'm tired of running away from what I feel for Chase. I'm tired of putting everyone in a bad position because I can't make up my mind. It has to end now, and end today.

She sighs and puts a hand to my cheek. “That's not going to be easy.”

“I know, but it will be right.”

27

———

I text Rhett on my way over to the apartment to let him know that we have to talk. I'm running on adrenaline right now, trying to think of what to say and how to say it. Telling him about Chase would only hurt him, and since I have no idea where Chase and I stand, I don't see any reason to bring him into the conversation. This is about Rhett and me. This is about how our relationship isn't what it should be, whether Chase is a factor or not.

I love Rhett. And I know he loves me. But the romantic love between us is gone. We're two different people going in two different directions. Sure, I could move to California with him and probably have a perfectly nice life. But there wouldn't be any magic. And I'm finally going to admit to myself that magic is something that I can't live without.

When I get to the apartment, Rhett is waiting for me. Most of the lights are off, so at first I don't see what he's holding. But when I do, my heart rushes into my throat.

"You went through my things," I whisper, staring at the photo in his hands. It's the picture of Chase that I took over ten years ago.

"You lied to me," he says, his voice eerily calm.

I take a step into the living room, unsure of how to respond. But faced with this evidence, I have to go with the truth. "Yes. I'm sorry."

His lips thin. "You both lied to me. Have you two been laughing behind my back this entire time?"

"Of course not," I breathe. "We would never."

"What else have you two been doing behind my back?"

"Nothing," I tell him. "I would never cheat on you."

"So when the two of you went on a secret trip to Vermont, you're saying nothing happened?"

I close my eyes. He knows about Vermont too.

"I'm sorry, Rhett. But Chase and I are just friends—"

"Bullshit!" he shouts, crumpling the picture in his hands and jumping up off the couch. "Do you think I'm stupid?! You don't think I saw how he looked at you and how you looked at him? I could tell something was up from the first night. Don't lie to me!"

"It's the truth," I insist, going to stand beside him. "Nothing has happened, I swear."

"What a shock it must have been," he says, laughing without humor. "Now your reaction on Thanksgiving makes sense. You saw a ghost!"

"Rhett, please. Calm down."

"He's been haunting our relationship for years. You weren't even going to date me in the first place because of him, so don't tell that nothing happened between you two. Something happened! How could you lie to me about this?!"

He slams a fist into the wall, making me jump.

"Because I was scared to tell you," I confess, tears filling my eyes. "I didn't plan for this to happen, and I didn't know how to deal with it—especially because he's working for you!"

"Not anymore. That deal is done."

My heart flies into my throat. "You can't do that!"

"I can do whatever the hell I want," he shouts, pointing a finger in my face. "I'm withdrawing all my funding, backing—everything. And I'll tell any investor who will listen to stay the hell away from his company."

"Rhett, you don't understand. His family is drowning in medical bills! They're counting on this money. They're counting on—"

"I was counting on you," Rhett shouts, glaring at me. "To not embarrass me and act like a ..."

My hackles go up. "Act like a what, Rhett?"

He doesn't respond, so I take the chance to go on the offensive. "That's just it, isn't it? You're embarrassed of me."

"Don't even go there."

"You want me to be your little trophy wife and run off to California and forget all my hopes and dreams."

"Forget all your hopes and dreams? What are you talking about? I always compliment your pictures."

"Yeah, and then you turn around and insult me by belittling my profession as a hobby."

"I'm sorry, but taking pictures is a hobby."

I put my head in my hands. "Rhett, can't you see that this isn't working between us? Chase aside, this relationship has been over for a long time. We don't want the same things."

His eyebrows fly up his forehead. "You're breaking up with *me*?!"

Tears fall down my cheeks. A part of me wants to tell him no. That somehow, we'll work it out. But I know that's only the fear talking. I have to listen to my heart, and do the right thing for everyone involved.

"This is over, Rhett. I think we both need to admit it. You should move to California and take that job offer. It's such a great opportunity for you. I want you to be successful and happy, more than anything, but I don't think that that will happen with me."

His chest heaves as he stares at me. "Just answer me this question, Birdie. And tell me the truth."

I blink away tears. "Okay."

He comes to stand before me, and I force myself to look him in the eye. "Do you love him?" he asks.

"I ... don't even know him," I whisper.

He shakes his head. "The truth, Birdie. Do you love him?"

I don't want to hurt Rhett. But I know in this moment, a lie will hurt more. So I hold his gaze while I admit the truth. "I think so. I think I always have."

Rhett's eyes close. Then with wooden steps, he walks back to the couch and puts his head in his hands.

I stand there, hating that I just gave him so much pain. I know in the long run this was something that had to happen. But if I ruined things for Chase and his business, and took away this opportunity from Rhett, I'd never forgive myself. I have to try for both of their sakes.

"Rhett," I begin. "Please don't stop working with Chase because of me. You both need this. And I—"

Rhett stands up, and I see him discreetly wipe a tear from his eye. "Don't worry. The investment was always safe. I can't go to California with an empty portfolio, and it's too late to find something else."

Relief floods me. But so does sadness. I want to run to Rhett and give him a hug, but I hold myself back.

Rhett gets up and heads for the hallway without looking at me. "You have an hour to get out of here. I'll move to my father's tomorrow, so you can have this place until the lease is up. But I can't look at you anymore tonight, so you need to leave."

Seconds later, our bedroom door slams shut. Long, heavy moments pass, but eventually, I'm able to get my feet to move. I leave the apartment quietly, wondering if I'll ever see Rhett again.

I think about calling Dasha and asking to stay at her place. Janice, of course, is no longer an option. She's obviously the one who told Rhett about Vermont, officially putting a wedge in our friendship that I don't think we can ever recover from.

I scroll through my phone and my finger stops on my mother's number. I'm just about to press it, but after the night I had, she's not the person I want to see.

In a daze, I start my car and drive slowly through the dark and quiet streets.

I have no idea if he's home. I have no idea how he'll react when he sees me. But I do know that there's nowhere else I'd rather be than with him. My soul is tethered to him, and I'm finally going to stop pushing against the current and let myself be where it should be.

It's late when I pull up to Chase's apartment and there aren't any lights on.

As I park in front of house, so many emotions are rushing through me. I'm scared, confused, excited, and so nervous that I feel like I'm buzzing.

Sucking in a breath, I stand on his porch and take out my phone.

I don't know why I don't want to knock. I think because I want him to know it's me before he gets to the door.

Birdie: I'm on your porch.

A minute later, I see the living room light turn on. Any

second now, he'll open the door, and things will change forever. So I close my eyes and breathe in this moment. I live in the anticipation. Because I know when we're standing face to face, there will be no going back for either of us.

28

"Birdie, what are you doing here?"

I open my eyes, bringing myself back to the present. Chase is standing in the doorway, shirtless. He looks me over, his face full of confusion.

I don't blame him. I was confused too.

But I'm not anymore.

I'm free. And I'm finally able to do what I've wanted to do since he's come back into my life. I should tell him that Rhett and I broke up. I should tell him that I want him, and what I'm here for. But as always, I can't find the right words. They're locked somewhere inside me, so I'll have to let him know in a different way.

With my eyes on his, I step forward and into his apartment. He backs up a few steps, scanning my face. "Birdie? Are you okay?"

I close the door behind me then turn to face him. There's only one dim light on, so he's cast in shadow, and it makes him look like something out of a dream.

He still looks confused, so I start unbuttoning my coat.

Still looking in his eyes, I drop it and my purse to the floor, then slip off my shoes.

"Birdie?" He goes to scoop them up, but then stops dead in his tracks as my hands go for the bottom of my shirt.

"What are you doing?" he asks, his voice breaking. His gaze locks on my hands, his own frozen in mid-air.

I respond by slowly pulling the shirt up and over my head. It isn't so much a strip tease as me laying myself bare.

Chase is breathing heavy now, and his hands are flexing by his sides. His eyes devour me slowly, as if cataloguing every new inch of skin that I reveal. But he doesn't move yet, and the intensity continues to swell until my hands start to shake.

So much so, it takes me a few more seconds than it normally would to unhook my bra.

Once that drops to the floor, Chase's face changes. The sheer desire that is in his gaze sends white-hot lust careening through my system.

He takes a step toward me. "I don't know what's happening right now," he whispers.

The strength of the moment is so profound, I almost can't bear it. But at the same time, I crave more of it. So I back up a step, just out of his reach.

My hands are on my pants next. I'm watching Chase, but he isn't looking at me. He's watching my hands again, and as I pull down my jeans, he makes a noise I've never heard him make before.

His eyes finally move back to mine. His jaw is slack and his gaze is full of a type of lust I've never seen before. It's more than sexual; it's visceral.

He's been so right all along. The chemistry between us is unmistakable. Otherworldly.

Magic.

I take a deep breath, fortifying myself to speak words before I even know if my voice will work. "Kiss me."

There's a pause. A pregnant beat. It's the sweetest little moment I've lived in so far.

And then he's coming toward me, his arms scooping me up with such force and ferocity I feel lightheaded.

And just before I close my eyes, I see the barest hint of that curved smile on his lips. It reminds me of the boy I met all those years ago. The smile that I carried and never forgot about.

That smile hasn't changed.

But his kiss ... his kiss is wildly different.

Gone is the awkward and hesitant boy, and in his place is a virile and confident man. The second our lips touch, everything frozen in me starts to melt. I could sing right now. I could talk about how I feel right now until my throat goes sore or I lose my voice.

I kiss him back with a fervor I didn't even know I was capable of, and his rhythm matches mine, as if we spent our whole lives kissing each other.

With each passing second, the kiss becomes better. No, not better—*more*. My whole being is now centered on where my lips are touching his, and the feeling is so indescribably wonderful, it brings tears to my eyes.

Chase pulls back, panting, then kisses a tear off my cheek I didn't even realize had fallen. "This is almost too much," he whispers.

"I know."

Our lips move together again before I even get the words out of my mouth. I don't feel in control anymore. My body is not mine; it belongs solely to this connection between us.

His body is so hard and warm. My legs wrap tighter around his waist, hoping to bring him closer.

His grip becomes tighter. "I want you."

"Then have me," I finally whisper back.

He pants against my lips and his eyes meet mine. "But what about—"

I don't want him to mention his name, so I kiss him in response to silence him. That should hopefully tell him all he needs to know.

"But what are we—"

"I'm on the pill and I'm clean. You?"

He nods. "Yes, but what I was going to say was—"

This time I make sure my kiss silences him.

And it works. Chase doesn't ask anything else. One of his hands is wrapped around my waist and the other around my back, and while he carries me into his bedroom, he squeezes me to him as if I'm the most precious thing he's ever carried.

His bedroom is cold, but when he places me on the bed and stands above me, the look he gives me sets my soul on fire.

"Is this really happening?" he asks, climbing on the bed. He straddles me, then reaches to grab both of my hands. He leans forward, holding down my arms above my head. "Please tell me this isn't a dream."

"If we are dreaming, let's get going so we don't wake up before the good stuff happens."

He laughs, and then his face changes so quickly, I wonder if the shadows are playing tricks.

"Why so serious?" I ask.

"Because I want to tell you something. But I don't know if I should."

"Then let's save the talking for later."

I arch my back up so my nipples press against his chest. He leans up and looks down at my breasts. He groans, then grinds into me, his face seeming almost pained.

"You're perfect," he says, sounding reverent.

He lets go of one of my hands and brings the other to his lips, kissing each fingertip gently.

"I want to kiss every part of you," he says.

So he does.

He starts at my palms and moves slowly to the heel of my hand. He gently kisses my wrist, then makes his way slowly down my arm, as if he has all the time in the world.

Knowing that it's Chase who's above me, worshipping me as if these are our last moments on earth, has me near mindless with pleasure.

"So soft. So smooth. You're so much more than perfect," he says, pressing kisses across my collarbone. He nips me under the chin, and I lean down, capturing his mouth for another searing kiss.

I want him so badly. More than I've ever wanted anyone. Reaching down between us, I try to grab for his cock that's been pressing up against my leg, but he stops me.

"No," he whispers. "I've waited too long. Let me taste you."

I moan, then nod, pressing my breasts against him again, letting him know that's where I need him. He complies, dropping his elbows to the bed and grabbing each of my breasts in his hands. His touch is rougher than his mouth was, and I cry out, writhing underneath him.

He laves both nipples in turn, sucking them hard into his mouth and then gently plucking them with his fingers.

Then he balances back up on the palms of his hands, staring down at me.

"Gorgeous," he says, shaking his head. "I can barely even look at you."

I groan, his words like kindling on my fire. Pressing my heels into the bed, I press my aching core against him. He presses back, and together we live in that short moment of unadulterated pleasure.

But then he pulls away and drops his mouth to my stomach. His tongue circles my belly button, then he presses open-mouth kisses all the way to the line of my panties.

"Please," I beg, needing his touch more than I need air. "Chase."

"Chase what?" he teases, kissing down the front of my panties.

When his mouth presses against my clit through the cotton barrier, I squeal with delight and frustration. "Chase, touch me, please."

I look down, and when our eyes meet, the arrogant half-smirk on his face is both sexy and annoying at the same time.

But he does what I ask and takes off my panties, dragging them off and tossing them to the floor as his eyes settle on the place between my legs.

He breathes heavy through his nose and says something under his breath, then descends down on me.

The first touch of his mouth feels like lightning, and I jerk with pleasure. He wraps his arms around my thighs, anchoring me to the bed as his mouth and tongue move over my clit and through my folds.

I'm so wet, and when I look down, his face is glistening with it.

One of his hands unwraps from my leg, and moves through the wetness to push inside me. My body bows off the bed and I cry out his name, unable to take the dual sensations.

But he doesn't stop. He manipulates and teases my body

into such a frenzy with his mouth and tongue, I feel like I'm balancing on a live wire.

"I'm going to come ..." I tell him, my voice strained.

I look at him, watching his muscles bunch as he pleasures me. And when his eyes meet mine, the orgasm that rushes through me feels like as large as a tidal wave.

My eyes shut as flashes of color dance on my eyelids. It feels like I'm getting a taste of heaven. And right as I'm cresting down, he pushes inside me and my back bows off the bed.

My core clenches around his length and I blink up at the ceiling, taking a moment to marvel at how beautiful it is to be filled by him. Chase groans low and long as he holds himself inside me, and I know he's doing the same thing.

He makes a noise and pulls back out, then slams back in even harder, making us both shudder. I've never had a moment like this, and I'm immediately scared that I never will again.

His elbows come down by my head as he continues to move in and out of me. Unable to keep still, I squirm and twist underneath him, pressing up every time he pushes in.

The sensation is indescribable, and I'm so wrapped up in it I barely notice that his mouth is against mine.

I try to kiss him back, but I'm so mindless with lust I feel uncoordinated. He has the same issues, and pretty soon our lips are just pressed together, as if they can't bear to not be touching.

Chase is big. Really big. And as his strokes start coming in fast and harder, I throw my head back open-mouthed on the bed.

"Nothing boring about missionary," he says under his breath. "Missionary is fucking amazing."

It takes me a second to figure out what he's referring to.

Then I remember Rhett's comment during King's Cup and almost laugh out loud.

He suddenly leans up to straddle me, then grabs both of my knees and pulls my legs apart.

And if I thought he was going hard and fast before, I was wrong. Dead wrong.

He pushes inside me as far as he can go, then he swivels his hips like a corkscrew, reaching some far distant part of me that I'm not sure has ever been touched before.

Another orgasm starts building inside me, and I reach up and grab his hands.

"I'm going to come ... again ..."

"Shit," he says, sweat dripping down his brow. "I don't know if I can last."

But he does. Just barely. The second tidal wave hits me hard and fast, and just as it peaks, Chase roars his release, pulling out and spilling himself all over me.

My body sinks into the bed, my chest heaving. My limbs are limp, lifeless, but inside I'm still burning, still on fire.

Chase's warm body settles on top of mine, and his hands brush my hair away from my face. He presses a light kiss to my lips, his breath coming as hard and fast as mine.

"That was ..." he says. "Something else."

I grin and kiss him back. "Yeah. It was."

He smiles and kisses the tip of my nose. "Be right back."

I watch him get up and head for his bathroom, my eyes locked on his ass the whole way. Did I really just have sex with this beautiful man? I think about all that's happened since he came back into my life. All the events that led us here. I'm scared, but inside I know that I'm changing. Maybe it's time to be brave and lean into that change.

Chase comes back with a warm washcloth. He crawls back into bed, then gently wipes my stomach. Once he's finished, he crawls back on top of me and frames my face with his hands.

"How is this happening right now?" he asks softly.

Even though I don't want to, I know I have to give him an explanation. "Rhett and I broke up."

His eyes go wide. "Are you serious?"

I nod. "Tonight. He found out about Vermont. Found that picture from when we were kids. And he knows who you are now."

"Shit."

"Don't worry. He's still planning on working with you. I made sure of it. It may be a little awkward but—"

"No, that's not it. I'm just worried about you. That must have been a difficult conversation."

I blink back tears. "It was. I don't know if I'm doing the right thing. It's just you ..." I scramble for the right words.

"Just me what?" he whispers against my lips. "Talk to me, baby. Tell me how you feel."

His voice, his touch, the way he's looking at me causes something inside me to melt just a little bit more. "I don't know if what I feel for you can be put into words."

"Want me to tell you how I feel?"

I nod just as he leans down and presses his lips against mine. My body sparks to life again, and I groan, moving under him. He makes a noise and bites my lip, grinding into me.

"I feel so happy," he says. "Like a kid on Christmas who has just gotten everything he's ever wanted."

His hardening cock rubs up against me, just short of slipping inside.

"I feel like the luckiest man on earth because I get to kiss the girl of my dreams, and touch her beautiful body."

I'm hearing what he's saying, but I'm losing focus fast.

What was I worried about, anyway? Nothing feels as right as this.

"And in the morning," he whispers, finally pushing inside me. "I'm going to ask her to be mine, so I can keep her forever."

And that's the last thing coherent thing I hear him say for a long, long time.

Chase makes love to me four times that night. And let's just say that now I know that rock n' roll is a real thing.

29

When I wake up the next morning, the bed beside me is empty.

Everything comes rushing back at once and the last twenty-four hours play like a movie reel in my brain.

Rhett and I broke up last night. Chase and I had sex. Lots and lots of sex. And he made me a vow right before he worshipped my body, over and over again.

He wants to keep me forever.

A part of me wants to panic. Life is changing and it's changing fast, and normally things like this give me whiplash. But as I lie there and wait for my anxiety to take over, I realize that I'm okay. Sure, I'm scared and nervous for what the future holds, but how can I regret what happened between Chase and me last night?

It was the most poignant experience of my life.

Full of moments that I could live in eternally.

But when Chase walks in a few seconds later, I take one look at his face and start to doubt myself. When he sees that I'm awake he tries to smile, but I can tell that something's wrong. His expression is tight, even though he's trying to hide it.

"What is it?" I ask immediately.

"It's nothing." He gets back into bed and pulls me into his arms. He puts his face in my neck and takes in a deep breath. "How did you sleep?"

I languish in his hold for a few seconds before pulling back. "Chase, what is it? I know something's wrong."

He sighs. "It doesn't matter, okay? This is what matters." He squeezes me tightly, as if to prove his point. "It's all that matters."

A dreadful feeling starts growing in my gut. "Chase, please. Just tell me. You're the one who's always pushing me to be honest. Now it's your turn."

He doesn't move for a few moments, but then he reaches over to his bedside table and grabs his phone. After pulling up a voice message, he hands it to me.

"Rhett called last night, but I just heard the message this morning."

I press play and put the phone to my ear, deep down already knowing what I'm about to listen to.

And sure enough, Rhett's familiar voice starts playing in my ear.

Closing my eyes, I listen as a furious Rhett tells Chase he's dropping him as a client. That their investment deal is done, the shop will be sold, and he's going to do everything he can to make sure that no other firm in the area will take on Chase and his business. I listen as Rhett tears Chase down as a man and calls him things I'm not sure I've ever heard Rhett say.

By the end of the message, I'm in tears. And when I do hand Chase back his phone, I'm full of regrets.

"I'm so sorry," I whisper. "This is all my fault."

"It's not your fault," he responds instantly. "He's upset. We can't blame him."

"He told me that he wouldn't do this. I should have known it was too good to be true."

He shakes his head, climbing on top of me. "We're too good to be true. This is too good to be true, okay? Don't fade out on me. I'm not going to lose you the second I finally have you."

"But you heard him," I say, a tear falling down my cheek. "Chase, your family … you need this money."

"I need you more."

"But what are you going to do?" I ask. "Your family was counting on this."

He takes a few deep breaths before answering. "I don't know, but I'll figure it out."

His words sound sincere, but I heard the pause in the beginning. He's scared. How can he not be? He doesn't have a plan, because he was banking on the money his bakery would make. I remember his words in the diner. And the hospital has already given him extra time. I'm suddenly so scared for him.

"Let me give you the money," I tell him, looking up and into his eyes. "I can ask my mom to borrow—"

"Absolutely not," he says.

"Chase, please, don't be proud about this. It's my fault Rhett is dropping you—"

"Birdie, I said no."

I sit up, dislodging him off me. "But why? I don't understand."

"Because money changes things between people. I grew up poor, so I know that better than anyone. Maybe down the line I would say yes, but not the second I have you back in my life. You and I are not starting out like that." He pushes me on my back and cages me in. "I've wanted you from the moment I met you. And now that I finally have you, I'm not letting a single thing come between us. Especially money. I refuse to let it taint what we have."

His voice is adamant and I know he's not going to change his mind.

But I have to help him. Just like he helped me all those Christmases ago.

"Now, let's drop it," he continues. "I'll figure something out, okay? Rhett's probably bluffing anyway. I'm sure there's another firm out there that will take me."

My heart sinks further. Rhett is not bluffing. He's not one to make idle threats. I want to tell Chase that, but I don't want to scare him. The wheels in my head are turning, however.

"Okay, let's drop it," I lie.

"Good."

He leans over and kisses me, and for a few more minutes, I let myself live in a fantasy.

30

When I leave Chase's house a few hours later, I'm determined.

Rhett isn't a bad guy. He can be reasoned with. I doubt he wants to hear me pleading Chase's case anymore, but I have to try.

Despite what Chase said, I saw the fear in his eyes. He did his best to hide it, but as connected with him as I am, I could see it lurking just underneath the surface.

How could Rhett do this? How could he be so callous? But of course, I answer my own question. He's heartbroken. He sees Chase as a man who came in and stole his girlfriend, and a part of me doesn't blame him for being upset.

Rhett told me that he was moving out today, but when I text him, he tells me he still hasn't packed up his things yet. I let him know that I want to talk, and then I hightail home as fast as I can.

When I get back to the apartment, he's there waiting for me, just like he was the night before. I don't know what I'm expecting. Anger? Sadness, maybe? But I see none of that. He's completely blank-faced.

"Where have you been?" he asks. I can hear the accusatory note in his voice.

I don't want to lie to him, but I can't tell him the truth either, so I just keep silent.

He scoffs. "You sure don't waste time, do you?"

Shame has my face turning red. "Rhett, you don't understand."

"Oh, I understand all right," he says, nostrils flaring. "You're completely done with me and you've already moved on. You don't love me anymore, and our whole relationship was a joke to you."

"It was not a joke," I say. "How can you think that?"

"How can you embarrass me like this?" he fires back. "How am I going to tell my dad what happened? That you dropped me for the ice cream man?"

"Don't call him that!" I shout. "And I don't care what you tell your father. This isn't just about you, Rhett."

"No, it's all about you," he says, throwing his hands up. "It's always all about you."

"It's about Chase too. You can't just drop him. He was counting on this money. You have no idea how much!"

"I was counting on you!" he yells. "I trusted you, and you went behind my back and screwed me over."

Guilt swarms through me. "I didn't plan for this to happen, Rhett, okay? I'm human, and I tried to deal with it the best I could. Can't you understand that? We had problems way before Chase came into our lives."

"I'll never understand," he says, voice cracking. I look up in surprise, shocked to see his eyes filling with tears. "Because I love you, Birdie. We were happy, weren't we? Sure, things weren't perfect, but it wasn't all bad, right? Was I bad to you? If I was, I'm sorry." The tears are sliding down his cheeks now, in full force. "I'm so sorry."

His vulnerability hits me right in the gut. I hate that I'm hurting him. It's the last thing I want to do.

"No, it wasn't all bad," I admit. "And of course you weren't bad to me. But there were things that just weren't working between us. I know you know what I'm talking about. We wanted different things."

"But we can work on those things and compromise," he says, coming to kneel in front of me. "Birdie, I can look past this Chase thing. I get it. I understand how much he meant to you, and I can accept it as a lapse in judgement. But can you really upend our whole lives for some guy you don't even really know? Can you really drop me like I'm nothing and kick me out of your life forever? After everything we've been through?"

He shakes his head, letting out a long breath. "I feel like you're abandoned me. We've been together for years and you're leaving me like I'm nothing. How can this be happening? How can you do this?"

His words hit me straight through the heart. He's right. Even though I know what I feel for Chase is real, what Rhett is saying is true. The second Chase came back into my life, I put my relationship with Rhett onto the back burner. I stopped working at it and I stopped trying. And in the process, I messed everything up for everyone.

Am I really that terrible of a person?

"Rhett, I'm sorry ... I didn't mean ..." I say, starting to cry.

I let him pull me into his arms, and I cry on his shoulder. I'm crying because either way, I don't win. No matter what, I hurt someone. It's a lose-lose situation for me.

Being with Chase last night, I felt things that I've never felt before. And thinking back on it now, it's clear as day that I'm in love with him. But if I choose him, I'm ruining things for him and Rhett. Chase's business goes under and Rhett's life is turned upside down. I'm the only selfish one who gets to reap the rewards.

But if I choose Rhett, life will continue on as it has been. I'll have to live without Chase, but at least his family will be safe and his business will be a success. He'll get over me eventually, especially when he realizes what he could have lost. Rhett will be happy, and I'm the only one who will have to live with a burden.

Maybe I'm fooling myself with that explanation, but it's clear to me it's the only path to take if I want to do the least damage.

But giving up Chase after last night? It feels impossible.

"It's okay," Rhett says, squeezing me tightly. "Just say you'll come back. Tell me we can forget this whole thing. Because I don't know if I can ever show my face around here ever again if we break up. I already told everyone I was proposing at the Christmas party."

My heart sinks to the pit of my stomach. It's nothing I didn't already know. But hearing him say it out loud is shocking and terrifying all at once.

I shake my head. "I don't want to hurt anyone."

"Then take me back. If you do, I promise I'll take Chase back on as a client. I'll call him right now. I didn't want to drop him anyway."

I lean back and look into his eyes. "Do you mean that?"

He nods instantly. "I promise. I'll even apologize. Just take me back and I'll do whatever you want."

A life with Rhett means a life without magic. But if it means Chase will be happy, I'll do it.

"Okay," I manage to get out.

He smiles at me and I force a smile back.

I wonder then how much of my life I'll have to spend forcing smiles.

31

The last thing I want to do is call Chase, but it's been a day since I've seen him, and I know I have to face the music.

Rhett told me that he called and accepted him back as a client. He said Chase was amicable, and that the whole thing is now behind them. Rhett also mentioned to me that he told Chase that he and I are back together, and I can only imagine what Chase is thinking.

He probably hates me now, and it's nothing less than I deserve. He probably thinks I'm a fickle, cruel-hearted woman. Maybe he's right. And I only have myself to blame. This whole mess is my fault and all I can do now is rebuild and start picking up the pieces.

I'm alone in the apartment, staring at the small moose picture I keep on my mantel. I wish my dad was here. He would know what to do. He was always so confident and strong, and sure of himself. He'd probably be so ashamed of the frozen and weak girl that I've become.

But it's time to be brave, so I press on Chase's contact

and hit send, shutting my eyes against the pain roiling around in my gut.

This is going to have to be goodbye. Because I don't think I can stand being just friends with Chase after the night we shared together.

The phone rings and rings, and I eventually I get his voicemail, which for some reason hurts even more.

He doesn't want talk to me, and I don't blame him. Not after what I did.

The thought of him hating me is so excruciating that when Dasha calls me a few minutes later, I'm sobbing.

"Oh, honey, what's wrong?"

The whole sad and terrible story comes out. I tell her everything that I'm feeling and what's been going on with both Chase and Rhett. I tell her the reasoning behind my decisions, and how much it hurt me to make them. By the time I'm done, I feel a little bit better, but my situation feels more permanent than ever.

"Birdie, Rhett is basically blackmailing you."

"It's not blackmail," I say, "because this whole thing is my fault. Why wouldn't he drop Chase after what I did to him? Who could blame him?"

"I can!" she says. "You need to do what makes you happy. And it sounds to me like being with Chase makes you happy."

"I'll be unhappy no matter what I choose. At least this way, I'm not destroying someone's livelihood and life in the process."

"I don't know," she says slowly. "I have a feeling this isn't going to end well. I'm scared for you."

"It can't get worse than it already is. Look, I'll be okay. Don't worry about me."

"I really think you should—"

"Dasha, please. This is hard enough. I really need you on my side here."

She sighs. I can tell she doesn't want to drop it, but luckily, she changes the subject. "Okay. Well, I was calling because you know what today is …"

"Yeah, I remember."

It's the twenty-third, which means I only have a few more hours to submit a photo to the holiday contest, and I have nothing.

"I don't have anything to submit," I tell her sadly. "I'm probably not even going to enter."

"You have to," she pushes. "Birdie, you're an incredibly talented photographer. You've taken a million pictures this past month. There has to be a gem hidden in there."

"There's not," I sigh. "There's nothing."

"Look again," she urges. "For me. Please?"

I want to refuse. Because I know that I don't have anything good. The best I can do is the moose picture, but submitting that somehow feels like a cop out. Dasha knows how much this contest meant to me—that's why she's pushing me—so for her, I'll do it.

"Okay, I'll look."

We get off the phone a few minutes later and I glance at the clock. I have an hour to choose something. I highly doubt I'll be able to find anything in time, but I grab my camera and start scrolling through anyway.

I skip through all the photos I took at Christmas town and around campus. I skip through the ones of Dasha, and the ones I took at the bed and breakfast.

There are some great shots in here, but nothing is right.

I start scrolling through the pictures in Vermont, and then I stop, unable to look away from the photo.

It's the one I took when Chase and I met up for a second

time in the woods. Chase is leaning against his thinking tree, decked out in his winter gear, silhouetted against a dusky winter sky. There's snow dotted on the ground around him, and in the distance are white-topped mountains.

But that's not what makes me look twice.

It's the expression on his face.

He looks deep in thought, but I can see the confusion and helplessness there. Anyone would look at this and think that he's unhappy.

But in the corner of his eye there's a spark of eagerness. A bit of hope in the small quirk to his mouth.

It's Chase as he is now. But I look at it and see the boy he was back then. Scared and confused, but so full of dreams that haven't yet been realized.

It's perfect.

At least, to me.

I quickly open my editing program and adjust the white balance and exposure, but otherwise, it's ready to go.

I submit the photo with a few minutes to spare, then take a picture and send it off to Dasha.

At least I've been able to do one thing right lately. The truth is, I don't feel the picture is a winner. But in my heart, I know it was the right submission for me, and that's all that matters.

I look up at the ceiling and smile, somehow feeling that this is something my dad would be proud of me for.

32

The venue Rhett chose for his Christmas Eve party is packed to the brim. The white and gold decorations make the whole room look like a winter wonderland. There are glittering icicles hanging from the ceilings, small ice sculptures in the middle of every table, and bright red champagne flutes made from what I know to be very expensive crystal. Rhett and his family went all out for this party, and everyone seems to be having a great time.

Everyone but me, that is.

"Sweetie, can you please talk to me?"

I take a sip of wine and look over at my mom. "Mom, I'm fine."

"You've barely said a word all night," she says softly. "And to be honest, I didn't expect to be coming to this party. Not after you told me you were ending things with Rhett."

I'll have to tell her the truth eventually. But right now, my emotions are way too raw. Chase never called me back, and I haven't seen him here tonight yet either. I look again over at the dessert table, but only a couple of workers Rhett must have hired are still setting up. There's no sign of Chase anywhere.

A part of me wants to go look for him—to see him and say goodbye face to face, and maybe try to explain things. But the cowardly part of me wants to avoid him. Because I don't think I can handle seeing the hurt on his face, even though I'm actually doing this *for* him.

"And do you want to tell me what's going on with you and Janice? Every time I look over, she's glaring in this direction."

"Mom," I sigh. "I promise I'll tell you everything. Just not tonight, okay?"

Because tonight I know I'll be facing Rhett's proposal. He all but confirmed it the other night, and I have to somehow play the part of the happy and surprised girlfriend. I don't think I have it in me, but I don't have a choice in the matter.

"Okay," my mom grumbles. "But—"

"Honey, why don't we grab another round of drinks?" Professor Donovan asks, touching her arm. "The Snowman Sangria looks delicious."

I shoot him a thankful smile. When my mom asked if she could bring him along, the little girl inside me wanted to say no. But my mom deserves to be happy. Who am I to stand in her way?

And now that I see them together, the connection they share is undeniable. They're so fluid. Their movements mirror each other one minute, then complement the next. It reminds me of my night with Chase. Even though it hurts to think about it now, I'm so selfishly glad that I have its memory.

Dasha comes over then and gives us all a big smile. "Room for one more?"

"Of course," I gesture to the chair next to me. "I've been saving you a seat."

She smiles, but it doesn't reach her eyes. And when she sits down, I know why. Checking to see my mom is distracted, she leans over and puts a hand on my leg. "I just saw Chase."

I try to act unaffected. "Oh? How did he look?"

"That's the thing ..." She looks at me with wide eyes. "He looked happy. He was joking around with his workers, and I think I even saw him whistling."

"Well ... that's good."

And shocking. I can't lie; hearing this information hurts. Even though I don't want Chase to pine over me, I did think he'd care a little bit. It's especially irksome considering he's not answering my calls. But maybe he understands the decision I made and is just relieved that his business is moving forward. I wouldn't blame him.

Dasha's eyes widen. "Shit. He's coming this way."

"What?!"

I turn just in time to see Chase kneel before me. He's in a Santa hat and a tux, and the smile on his face is as jolly as Old Saint Nick himself.

"Hey, beautiful," he says grabbing my hands. "Sorry I haven't called you back. I've been up over my head getting ready for this party. Don't want to push Rhett more than we already have, you know?"

I mouth at him, unsure of what's going on. "Chase, I ..."

"I don't know what you told him, but I wanted to thank you. He called me and told me he overreacted. And said that if we wanted to be together, he wouldn't stand in our way."

Dasha gasps beside me. I stare at Chase, black and oily panic settling into my gut. "Chase, I don't think you understand."

"Shit, I have to go," he says looking over my shoulder. He brings both of my hands to his mouth and kisses them. "I just wanted to come over to tell you that you look absolutely beautiful, and I can't wait until later, when I can kiss you endlessly. I can't believe we finally get to spend our first Christmas together."

His words are so surprising and unexpected, I let him get up and walk away without saying anything.

"I don't understand," I whisper to Dasha.

But as soon as the words are out of my mouth, my eyes catch Rhett's over her shoulder. He's staring at us with a dark smile on his face, and I know that he saw the whole exchange with Chase. And now I know exactly what's going on.

"Oh, God." I turn to Dasha. "Rhett did this on purpose. He wants Chase to witness the proposal."

"What?" Dasha's hand covers her mouth. "But why would he do that?"

"Because he wants to hurt him. He wants to embarrass Chase like Chase embarrassed him."

But I also think that it's not only about that. I think Rhett wants to punish me. As far as Chase knows, we spent a night together and Rhett is out of the picture. In his mind, Rhett is being the bigger man about the situation and letting me go quietly. He thinks Rhett has admitted to overreacting and is excited to get the business back on track.

But Chase doesn't know Rhett like I do.

"Should I warn him?" Dasha asks.

"I'll do it. It should come from me."

But just as I'm getting out of my seat, the sound of Rhett's voice fills the room.

"Good evening, ladies and gentlemen ... if I could please have your attention for a moment."

Rhett is standing on the dance floor, a bright smile on his face. Gone is the darkness I saw earlier. A voice in my head whispers that I should run, but instead I find myself frozen—glued to the spot.

"I hope you're all enjoying your evening, and that you've had a glass of our Snowman Sangria, courtesy of the talented Mr. Chase Cyrus."

My eyes close. He's twisting the knife. He wants Chase's attention on what he's going to say next. Putting a hand on my stomach, I sink into my seat. I feel ill. This can't be happening.

"Birdie?" my mom asks, the worry in her voice evident. "Are you okay?"

I don't respond. Because I'm not okay, and I don't know that I ever will be again.

"Now, the holidays are a time for family," Rhett continues, pacing the floor. "Which is why Christmas has always had a special place in my heart, because to me, nothing is more important than family. And yes, Branson, it's even more important to me than the Patriots."

Chuckles fill the air. Someone puts a hand on my back as his words start a low hum in my ear.

"But this year in particular, I'm hoping that family will mean something new. It feels like this girl has already been a part of my family, but I finally want to make it official. Beatrice Anne Tenneson ..."

My eyes instinctively go to Chase. He's staring at Rhett, and I can see the wheels in his head turning. And then I see those wheels come to a dead and painful stop, and when I turn back to the front of the room, Rhett is on one knee.

"Would you do me the greatest honor and become Mrs. Rhett Branholder?"

The cheers and catcalls start before he even finishes his

sentence. My eyes go to Chase again, and this time he's looking at me. He's searching my face, looking for answers. He doesn't understand what's going on, and is terrified I'll say yes. Because that's what I see after searching his face. Pure and abject terror.

It almost makes me confident enough to say no—to refuse Rhett in front of all these people, and then run into Chase's arms and start a new life. But I can't do that. Because if I do, Chase will have me, but he'll lose everything he's ever worked for. Even if he did accept money from me, he'd lose all of Rhett's assets and connections and his shop would fail. I'm still in the lose-lose situation. Nothing has changed.

And why would Chase want someone like me anyway? A frozen girl who lets life happen to her, instead of the other way around.

I feel like I'm about to panic, so I close my eyes. I slow down and live in this moment. Not because it's a good one, but because it's my last moment of freedom.

When I open them, there's a smile on my face. My feet start moving toward the dance floor, and my head is nodding. I can't say yes. I can't physically say the word. But when I reach Rhett and he pulls me into his arms, my meaning is clear.

Something smashes behind me, but it's drowned out by the cheering and shouted well-wishes. But I heard it all the same, and I know that it was Chase.

I wish he knew I was broken just as badly.

Rhett pulls back and grabs my hand, sliding what I know is a massive ring onto my finger. I don't look down at it. I don't have a chance before he smashes his lips against my own. He's kissing me like a victor—like he knows he's won.

Before this, I would have been content with Rhett. I

always would have thought about Chase, but I was willing to accept and settle, knowing Chase was fine and I wasn't abandoning anyone in the process.

But now, after what he did to Chase—and what he did to me—I can't stomach his touch.

This is wrong. So wrong.

The next few minutes pass by in daze. Rhett's dad comes over and calls me his daughter, and I smile through it. Strangers shake my hand and make jokes, and I laugh like I should. But the second I can get away, I do. I squeeze Rhett's hand, tell him I have to use the restroom, then book it out of there.

33

My senior prom was held at this venue, so I remember an out-of-the-way bathroom that the staff and caterers usually use on the bottom floor. I head for it, not wanting to be bothered.

Once inside, I drop onto the old pink couch and put my head in my hands.

I'm furious with myself. I let myself get caught up in this mess, all because I was too afraid to say how I feel. All because I'm frozen, per usual.

The door creaks open and when I look up, it's the last person I expect to see.

"Congratulations," Janice says, smiling at me.

She walks over and grabs my hand, turning it this way and that, eyes on the ring. I see now that it's a very large pear-shaped diamond. It's beautiful, but it's not something I would have chosen for myself.

"That was quite the proposal," she continues, walking over to look in the mirror. "Was that magical enough for you? Or was it missing a sprinkling of fairy dust?"

I stare at her in shock. This is a girl who I've known for years and who I've called a best friend, and she's treating me like I'm her sworn enemy. I think about getting up and walking away, and not responding to her at all. That's what I would have done before.

But things are different now. Maybe living through this miserable proposal and everything that happened with Chase has made me braver. Maybe it's dislodged the words from my throat that I should have said long ago. Whatever it is, it has my feet moving, and I don't stop until I'm standing directly in front of her.

"What happened to you?" I ask.

She turns to me, her lip curled. "What's that supposed to mean?"

"You're bitter, angry, jealous, and mean. And I know it was you who told Rhett about Vermont. Was that to try to break us up? Why would you do that to me?"

She glares at me. "Because you're so damn ungrateful! You have everything. And you don't seem to give a damn about the things you have to treat them with any care."

"If you think I have everything, then you don't know me at all."

She scoffs, the sound echoing off the old tiles. "Spare me the 'woe is me' act. You've had two amazing guys pining over you this past month, and you've been walking around in your designer clothes like you're the unluckiest woman in the world. You've been unbearable to be around."

I glare at her. "My designer clothes? What is that supposed to mean? Are you saying that because my family has money, I'm not allowed to feel sad? Or angry? Or confused? What's really going on here, Janice? And tell me the truth."

She looks away, her tears filling her eyes. "Just go away."

"Not until you tell me what's going on. Please. I want to help."

She turns to me, her eyes flashing. "I don't want or need your help. Now how about you and that ring get out of my face?"

My whole body tenses, anger infusing my every limb. "You know what? I will. Because even after everything you did to me, I was still willing to listen to you. Still willing to help if you needed it. But no more. That was all I had left. You've turned into a toxic, angry woman, and I want no part of it. You're a bitch, Janice. A bitch. And this friendship is over."

I'm just about to walk out the door, when Janice's quiet voice stops me. "Rhett was supposed to be mine."

I turn and stare at her, stunned. "What?"

"You met Rhett at *my* Christmas party. I met him before-hand at the library and we hit it off, so I invited him. He and I had been flirting all night before you showed up. There was a spark between us, and it seemed like the stars were align-ing. Everything was going to be perfect. But then he saw you and of course, just like everyone else, he fell at your feet."

Shock pulses through me in heavy waves. "Janice, you never told me that."

"I never wanted to say anything, because you were my friend, but I can't tell you how many hours I spent wondering—if you never showed, would I be the one wearing that ring right now?"

"I ... I don't know what to say."

She shakes her head, looking down at my ring. "One thing's for sure. I would have appreciated it. It would have meant the world to me. This past month, watching you throw it all away has made me ..." She lets out a heavy breath, her expression morphing into something angry and bitter. "It's just so damn unfair."

"Yeah, it is unfair. Because you're punishing me for something I had no idea about. Why are you even telling me now?"

"I just need to get it off my chest. I just want you know why I've been so angry lately."

"You've been more than angry. You've been acting like you hate me."

Her lips quiver. "I know. And I'm so sorry. I just ... I think a part of me does."

A heavy weight falls between us and I feel a lump growing in my throat. I follow her gaze down to my ring. A symbol of what is supposed to be love, but has caused so much heartbreak, including hearts that aren't my own.

This stupid ring. It's so big and gaudy, it feels more like an anchor.

"I'm sorry. I wish things didn't happen this way," I say. I take off the ring, feeling its weight in my hand. "We should talk about this later. Or, you know what? Maybe we won't. Either way, I need some space."

Janice wipes a tear, looking away. I stand there for a moment, wondering if I should just break down and ask if we can put this behind us, but I can't. I can't be that person ever again. So after a few more seconds, I turn and leave the bathroom.

The hallway outside the bathroom is dark, and once I find a small alcove, I sneak into it and drop to the floor. I should probably go back. I need to talk to Rhett and tell him that things are over between us. That I never should have said yes.

I want to talk to Chase too, but I know he'll never forgive me. I don't deserve his forgiveness. Not after what I did.

"Sweetie?"

I look up and my mom is standing above me. Seeing the concern on her face is my undoing, and I burst into ugly tears.

"Oh, Birdie," she says, sinking down on to the floor beside me. "Please don't cry."

"I can't help it," I sob. "I've ... I've ruined everything."

"That can't be true," she says, pulling my head onto her shoulder.

"But it is ..."

I tell her about what happened with Chase and Rhett—about how he set this whole thing up, and how now I've gone and hurt Chase more than I wanted to.

She holds me close to her side and lets me cry it out.

"I never should have said yes to Rhett," I tell her. "I knew it was wrong, but I couldn't stand the thought of ruining Chase's life."

"I don't think you've ruined his life," she says. "It sounds like he was willing to give up everything for you."

"I didn't deserve it then, and I don't deserve it now. It's too late."

She pulls back and frames my face with her hands. "It's never too late to do the right thing."

I nod, but I don't agree with her.

Wiping my face with my hands, I try to pull myself together. I have to face Rhett and tell him that our engagement is off. But just as I go to stand, my phone pings.

It's an email notification. The results of the Holiday Contest.

A part of me wants to drag the whole thing out —

maybe ask my mom to open it. But I'm done being a coward, so with shaking fingers, I open the email and read the results.

I get to the name of the winner, and for the first time all night, I smile.

34

I search for Rhett everywhere, but he's nowhere to be found.

It's not like him to disappear from his own party, and I can't help but wonder if something is wrong. After leaving the main room, I grab my coat and head outside, worried that something might have happened.

Did he confront Chase? Did Chase confront him?

I hurry my steps, searching the grounds, but the lot is empty.

I pass by his car, then stop short.

He's in the driver's seat, staring straight ahead. His hands are on the steering wheel, and I'm shocked to see that it looks like he's been crying.

I walk around to the passenger side and after a moment's hesitation, I open the door.

"Rhett?" Shutting the door behind me, I turn to face him fully in the seat. "I need to talk to you."

"I already know what you're going to say."

I bite my lip, tears forming in my eyes. "I can't marry you. I'm sorry."

He doesn't respond until the silence becomes almost unbearable. "I know."

"I just can't pretend that—"

"I don't blame you," he cuts in. "Not after what I did to Chase. And you."

Even though I'm mad at him, the hurt in his voice breaks my heart. "Why did you do it?"

He laughs without humor. "Because I couldn't let him beat me. That's the main reason why. I couldn't see past my huge stupid ego to realize that I was also hurting you." He finally turns to me. The look he gives me is full of meaning. "And that's why you're better off with him. Because my reasons for keeping us together are all about myself. His reasons will always be about you."

I shake my head, crying. "I'm sorry, Rhett. I never wanted to hurt you."

He nods and wipes his nose. "I know." His hands grip the steering wheel and he straightens up as if gathering himself. "I'm going to move to California."

I nod. "I think you should. I mean, don't take that the wrong way, but you were right. It's an opportunity of a lifetime."

"Yeah. Thanks."

He turns and gives me a sad smile, and I give him one back. I don't feel like smiling, and I doubt he does either, but I think we both know that it's the last time we're going to see each other for a long, long time, and it's the least we can do as we pull apart the pieces of our lives that have been entwined together for years.

"I'm not going to invest with Chase," he says. "The equipment's already paid for, so he can keep it all. I'll offer to sign over full ownership of the shop, but he has to pay for it from now on. I can't give him any more of my money. And

I can't handle that kind of constant working relationship with him."

"I understand."

I grab the door handle, then remember something and turn back. "This is going to be hard for both of us, and I bet you'll need a shoulder to lean on as much as I will. You should call Janice."

He turns to me, confused, but I let the statement hang as is.

When I get back inside, I head for the dessert table. I don't expect Chase to forgive me. But even though I don't expect that it will help anything, I can't leave tonight without apologizing.

My heart sinks, however, when I see that the dessert table has been upended. That explains the crash I heard earlier. I approach the young boy who has unfortunately been tasked with cleaning everything up. I bend down and start to help.

"Is Mr. Cyrus still here?" I ask quietly.

The boy looks up and shakes his head. "No. He just threw this table and then told us he had to be back home in Vermont for Christmas, then left. I don't know what his problem was."

Chase is gone. He went back to Vermont, and I don't blame him.

I help the boy pick up the rest of the mess, then head for the exit.

I can't remember a Christmas where I've felt so miserable.

But as I walk to my car, tears fill my eyes.

Because actually, I can remember one other one.

35

———

That night I dream of moose.

Not the majestic, serene creature I saw in Vermont with Chase, but an angry moose that's kicking down my door. I scream, watching as the wood splinters around me. The moose doesn't look normal. It's bright red and the eyes look more human than animal. It starts running toward me, and I cover my eyes and brace myself for impact.

I wake up, screaming and covered in sweat.

What the hell was that all about?

I put my head in my hands, trying to catch my breath.

It's then that I realize I'm still in my gown from the Christmas party. I came home to my mom's and cried myself to sleep, and I must have passed out sometime around midnight.

A look at the clock tells me it's three a.m.

It's Christmas.

I look at the door, imagining the painted moose barreling through it. The moose was angry, but I can't imagine why. What a strange dream.

I get out of bed and walk over to the window, remembering how much my dad loved moose. He loved Christmas too. I touch my necklace, rubbing it between my fingers and thinking of the day I found it.

Putting my hand on the glass, I think of his words.

Christmas Eve is a night for magic.

And Christmas is a day for miracles.

My hand pauses on the glass, but just for a moment. Because then I start scrambling around the room, getting dressed as fast as I can.

It doesn't take me long to drive to Vermont.

It's early Christmas morning, so there's no one on the road. I call my mom from the car and explain why I won't be at her house, and instead of being disappointed, her enthusiasm for my plan gives me hope.

I need hope.

Because if I'm going to get Chase to forgive me, I really do need a miracle.

I drive to Mistletoe Cabin and park on the side of the street, and then I walk through the woods to the thinking tree. I don't expect to see Chase there, but I'm hoping that if I stay there long enough, he'll come by. I still have no idea where he lives, and I wish like hell I had asked when we were up here.

The woods are quiet, serene, and dotted with snow, and I take a couple of deep breaths, feeling like each one clears my head a little bit more.

When I make it to the tree, I smile. I should have known I wouldn't have to wait long. Now that I've seen magic, I know that anything is possible.

Chase is on the ground, staring ahead, and for a moment, I drink him in. From the curl on his forehead, to the contemplative, sad expression on his face. He's so distracted that he doesn't know I'm there yet. So after gathering my courage, I take a step forward.

"Happy birthday," I whisper.

His head shoots up, surprise filling his face. "Birdie? What are you doing here?"

I lift up the envelope. "I have a gift."

He stares at me for long moments, then looks away in anger. I expect him to lash out at me. To yell and scream and blame me for ruining his life. But he doesn't do any of those things. He just stares ahead blankly and silently, which is ten times worse.

"I didn't know ..." I tell him. "That Rhett hadn't told you the truth. I didn't know he was going to do that."

He still doesn't say anything, so I soldier on.

"When I left your house after our night together, I didn't plan on getting back with Rhett. I just wanted to try to fix things so you could continue working together. But he wasn't going to budge unless I got back together with him. So I said yes because I didn't want to ruin your life."

He scoffs, shaking his head. "You didn't want to ruin my life, huh?"

Tears form in my eyes. He really does hate me. "I'm sorry. I'm so sorry—"

"Don't you get it?" he says, standing up. "You're the only thing I've ever wanted in my life. It was true when I was a kid, and it's true now as an adult. You ruined my life by walking out of it. Because nothing else matters. Not the money, not the business, not anything. I would have found a way to take care of my family. But I'll never find a way to replace you."

"I'm sorry, I just ... I couldn't have lived with myself if I was the reason your dream collapsed. If I was the reason your family—"

He shakes his head, backing away. "You didn't need to come all this way just to tell me that. Go home, Birdie."

His words are like a knife to the heart, but I have to keep trying. For the life of me, I cannot freeze right now. "That's not why I came here," I say quietly.

"Then why did you?"

"I'm hoping for a miracle."

He blinks at me, cocking his head to the side. "What?"

I take a step toward him. "We already have the magic. Now I want the miracle."

"I don't understand what you mean."

I hand him the envelope. "Open it."

After a beat, he reaches out and takes it from my hands. He opens it, and when he sees what's inside, he looks up, confused. "What is this?"

"It's the picture I chose for the Holiday Photo Contest."

"You chose a picture of me?"

I step toward him until we're mere feet apart. "I had to find the perfect picture to represent Christmas, the most wonderful time of the year—my favorite time of the year. You are the perfect embodiment of what Christmas means to me. You have been since that night."

He shakes his head, tears filling his eyes. "Birdie, what are you saying?" His brow suddenly furrows, and then he reaches down to grab my hand. He feels around on my finger, then looks back up at me. "Where's your ring?"

"Back with Rhett, where it belongs."

His jaw drops as he realizes what I'm telling him.

"I never should have said yes to him. Chase, I know we've only known each other as adults for a couple of weeks, but I feel like I've known you all my life. You've shaped my life. And I want you to know that I love you. I missed my chance to say it to my dad back then, and I won't make the same mistake twice."

He stares at me, his eyes shining. And then I'm suddenly wrapped up in his arms, and then he's kissing me, whispering "I love you" to me over and over. He kisses me like his life depends on it, and now I know that it does. It's the same for me, so I kiss him back just as passionately, as relief, desire, and happiness fill me from the inside out.

His lips against mine feel like a miracle. Somehow, I found it on Christmas morning. And when we pull back, we're both smiling.

"I love you," I say again, looking into his eyes. "I fell in love with you that night years ago, and I've loved you ever since."

His eyes lock on mine and he pulls me close. "I love you too. More than anything else in the world. If I have you, then I know that everything will be okay."

I hate that worry is creeping in at a moment like this, but I can't help it. So I tell Chase the information I know he needs to hear. "Rhett said he'd sign over rights to the shop and let you keep the equipment. Is that enough?"

He presses a kiss against my lips. "It's a start, but I don't know how I'll pay the rent."

"I do."

The feminine voice has us both jumping with shock. I jump again when Dasha steps out of the woods with a big smile on her face.

"Dasha," I cry, running over to her. "What are you doing here?"

"I got a call from Aunt Marlene this morning, telling me where you were." She crosses her arms. "I didn't want you to be alone on Christmas—or, God forbid, heartbroken—so I followed you."

I pull her into my arms. "You didn't have to do that."

"Yes, I did. And I'm glad I did. Because this year, I can finally give you the perfect gift."

"Dasha ..."

I don't want to be rude, but I really don't care about gifts right now. As if she can read my mind, she holds up a hand and turns to Chase.

"Chase, what are you doing with that empty room in the back of your shop?"

Chase sputters, looking at me. "I don't know. Extra storage, I guess."

"Would you be willing to rent it out to Birdie and me?"

"What?" I shake my head. "Dasha, what are you talking about?"

"Isn't it obvious?" she says, smiling. "If we rent out Chase's back room as a work space, we can help him with rent."

Chase comes over to stand beside us. "Dasha, that's really sweet of you. But so much more goes into it. The first few months I'd be operating at a loss and—"

"That's where the gift comes in."

She reaches into her pocket and pulls out a five-thousand-dollar check. She smiles, handing it out to me. "Merry Christmas. This should help with rent for the first three months. After that, your shop will be raking in cash and you'll be able to afford it. Especially with me and Birdie renting out the back room."

I stare at her, stunned. "Dasha, I can't accept this!"

"You can and you will."

"But—"

"I've been telling you for years that I want to give you the perfect gift. And now I finally have."

"Money?" I question.

"No," she says, smiling. "I'm giving you Chase's happiness."

Her words flow through me and cut straight to the heart. "Dasha, I don't know what to say."

"Say yes," she replies, grinning. "Besides, look at it as a payment for using your image."

We both laugh, but Chase holds up a hand. "What does she mean, your image?"

I put an arm around Dasha. "Dasha won the Holiday Photo Contest with a photo she submitted of me. It was gorgeous work, so the title was completely well deserved."

"And this check is my prize money and a little extra, which I'm giving to you two."

"I ... thank you," he says, looking up at Dasha. "Thank you so much. But the only way I can accept this is if I can see this as a loan. Can I pay you back?"

"As far as I see it, if you keep Bird and I supplied with delicious coffee and snacks throughout the day, we can call it even."

Chase stares at her blankly. I shift my feet, realizing that for him five thousand dollars is a lot of money. I give her a look and shake my head slightly.

Dasha smiles. "If it really matters to you, then yes, you can reimburse me when the bakery hits it big. I know it will."

Chase looks at me and I see hope in his eyes. Without another word, he pulls Dasha and me both into a hug.

I close my eyes to slow down time. I live in this wondrous, joyous moment, where I'm hugging two of the most important people in my life, and all of us are looking toward a bright future.

When we pull back, Dasha looks behind us. "So this is the infamous tree, huh?"

"This is it," I say, stepping into Chase's arms.

"It's beautiful. And it does look magical." She looks around, then smiles. "Maybe if I look hard enough, I'll find some too."

We all laugh, then Dasha repositions us so we're standing in front of the tree. "We need a picture of the three of us to commemorate this moment. I'll set my camera up over there and—"

"I can take it."

All three of us turn toward yet another new voice. A beautiful brunette comes out of the trees, smiling at Chase.

"Cammy?" Chase asks. "What are you doing here?"

"Dad was hoping to get Christmas breakfast started. We were wondering where you were." She turns to Dasha and me and waves. "Hi. I'm Chase's sister, Cameron."

"Hi," I say, moving forward to shake her hand. "I'm Birdie."

Her eyes widen. "*The* Birdie?"

"The very one." Chase grins. He leans down to peck my lips. "Cammy, this is my girlfriend." His chest puffs out with pride.

I look up at him, my heart soaring in my chest.

"And this is Dasha," Chase says. "Birdie's cousin."

I look over and see that Dasha's cheeks are bright red. I smile to myself. I know that look. Dasha has got a major, serious crush. And from the way Cameron is looking at Dasha, I'd say she's not the only one.

"Both of you are invited to my house," Chase says happily. "We'll all celebrate Christmas together."

Everyone starts talking at once. And as we head into the forest toward Chase's house, something in the distance catches my eye.

It's very far away this time, and it's dark still, because the sun hasn't completely risen, but I swear there's a large, majestic creature standing in the forest. The snow around him sparkles and gives off a magical twinkling effect.

I stop and smile at the moose, knowing my dad is watching over me.

Chase stops beside me. "Are you okay?"

I turn to him, then lean on my toes and kiss his lips. "I'm perfect."

"Congratulations, Chase! You've outdone yourself."

Chase grins, shaking Professor Donovan's hand. "Thanks, Henry. This has been a dream come true."

From across the room, I stare at Chase, who is surrounded by his well-wishers.

It's Christmas Eve and we're in Vermont, celebrating the opening of Chase's second shop. The one in New Haven was such a success that he was able to start drafting plans for this one within six months of opening.

It's been a crazy six months, but Chase insisted on opening on Christmas Eve. A date that means so much to both of us.

Next to me, Dasha is snapping pictures. But not the pictures she's supposed to be taking.

"Dasha," I start, amused. "You're supposed to be taking pictures of the opening."

"I know, but she's so beautiful." Dasha grins, then takes another photo of Cameron. "Isn't she so beautiful?"

I laugh, over-the-moon happy for her. The two shared their first kiss last New Year's Eve, and they've been inseparable ever since. The four of us spend a lot of time together, especially now that Cameron's moved to Connecticut.

I hear Chase's laughter, and I look over to see him hugging his father. His dad will be running this shop up in Vermont, and I swear, the position breathed new life back into the old man. Speaking of new life—

I put a hand on my stomach, excitement rushing through me. I'm going to tell Chase the good news tonight when we're back in our room at Mistletoe. It will be the perfect anniversary, birthday, and Christmas present, and I know how excited he's going to be.

"Birdie?"

I look over just as my mom walks up. "Hey, Mom."

"This package was just delivered at the front of the shop."

I take the small box from her hand. "Who's it from?" I ask.

She smiles, putting a hand on my arm. "It's from California."

My heart flies into my throat, and I move to the side of the room and open the box. When I see what's inside, I gasp. It's a miniature version of Chase's New Haven shop, made out of glass. It's decorated for Christmas, and the name of the shop—Melt—is written in cursive across the top.

"What's that?"

I turn just as Chase comes up beside me. "A gift. From Rhett and Janice."

Chase smiles, picking up the miniature. "This is amazing. We'll have to display it somewhere in the shop."

"It is."

Janice and I talked briefly over text for the first time a month ago. Long story short, she and Rhett are now together and living together in California. They seem happy, and I'm happy for them. I don't know if I'll ever have a relationship with either one of them again, but I guess we can never say never.

Chase pulls me into his arms. Then he grabs my hands and kisses the emerald ring on my finger. "Next Christmas, you'll be my wife."

That won't be the only thing that'll be new next Christmas. I almost tell him the news now, but I want to wait until midnight. And I want to do it at our tree.

Overwhelmed with happiness, I reach up and press my lips against his. He sighs happily into my mouth, wrapping his arms around me. We don't pull back until we hear a catcall from across the room.

We laugh, then look back into each other's eyes.

"Merry Christmas, Birdie."

"Merry Christmas. And by the way, you're not a bad kisser."

SNEAK PEEK OF LOVESICK, ELLE & STEVE'S STORY

Chapter 1

"Elle, I'm telling you this as your best friend. This is a really bad idea."

Nikki's words come through the phone loud and clear, but they don't register. Because I'm set on my plan. I've been hooking up with Tom Allen for exactly one month, and tonight I'm going to surprise him. I place one final balloon by his bed, then adjust the "Happy Anniversary!" sign I taped to the headboard.

"I know what you're thinking," I tell her. "And I know Tom and I aren't official or anything. But once he knows how I feel, all of that is going to change." Loud footsteps suddenly sound from the hall. "Got to go! He's here."

"But—"

I end the call and jump on Tom's bed. The door opens, and the speed of my already racing heart ratchets up a notch. When his blond head finally appears, I throw my hands in the air. "HAPPY ANNIVERSARY, TOM!"

He jumps back at the sound of my voice. He looks at me,

then around the room, in shock. "Elle? What are you doing here?"

I climb off the bed and give him my biggest smile. "I wanted to surprise you. I know we don't usually see each other during the week, but I thought it'd be okay to make an exception. You know, since today is our one-month and all."

I gesture to the sign and my T-shirt. Both proclaim the happy message. But the look on his face morphs into one of horror, and laughter sounds from behind him. It's then I notice that he's not alone. His frat brothers are here too, and it's clear they're enjoying the drama. My smile starts to falter. I look back at Tom, whose face has gone hard.

"Elle, we're not dating," he snaps.

"Not yet, but—"

His nostrils flare. "Not ever. I know I made that clear. I told you I wasn't looking for a relationship."

"Right, but I thought..." I trail off when I realize the laughter outside the room is only growing louder.

Tom stomps over to the headboard and rips off the sign. "Whatever you thought was wrong. I call you on the week-ends, we fuck, and that's it. That's all this is. I mean..." He swipes his hand over the bed, pushing the scattered rose petals to the floor. "Are you serious with all this shit?"

My lower lip starts to tremble, and humiliation burns through me like battery acid. I thought this thing between Tom and me was different. I thought we really connected. But Nikki was right. This was a bad idea. I was misreading the situation, just like I always do.

Tom rolls his eyes at my expression. "Great. Now I'm the bad guy. You know, I heard around campus you were a little crazy. A stage-five clinger. I ignored it because of how hot you are, but joke's on me, I guess."

I start backing away, knowing what's coming next. I don't want to hear it.

His eyes narrow on mine. "You and I? We're done."

I turn and make a beeline for the door. I hate those two stupid words. I've heard them time and time again, from guy after guy. I'm so flustered that I bump into someone on my way out. I look up and into the eyes of Steve Towers, and my stomach sinks further. Figures I'd embarrass myself in front of one of the most popular guys on campus.

When I see his expression, I don't stop to apologize. Because if there's anything worse than rejection or laughter, it's pity.

ABOUT THE AUTHOR

Kayla Parent lives in Massachusetts with her swoon-worthy husband Jimmy, her sweet son Garrett, and her mischievous beagle, Gus. When she's not writing, she's reading. She's enamored with historical romance, contemporary romance, folk tales and true-life crime. She's also a self-proclaimed champagne enthusiast, a chronic daydreamer, and popcorn fanatic.